H₂O

H₂O

Irving Belateche

Laurel Canyon Press
Los Angeles

Laurel Canyon Press, October 2012

H_2O

ISBN: 978-0-9840265-2-4

Library of Congress Control Number: 2012916044

Cover design by Karri Klawiter
Cover design based on the painting "Seal Rock 2" by Albert
Beirstadt
www.artbykarri.com

Layout provided by Everything Indie
www.everything-indie.com

Laurel Canyon Press
Los Angeles, California
www.LaurelCanyonPress.com

www.irvingbelateche.com

Chapter One

THE PHONE RANG, waking me up from a deep sleep. The kind of sleep where you don't have a past or future, just a murky present that you don't quite understand. It was Frank and he wanted me down at the plant. A pump in one of the pumping stations had broken down and I was next in line to fix it.

That I understood.

But as I dressed, I tried not to think about it.

I was always thinking too much so I turned this into yet another test of whether I could stop. I couldn't. I knew that fixing that pump meant heading out into the wilderness and I knew that heading out into the wilderness meant heading out to die.

I DROVE UP the rugged coast toward the desalination plant. It was twenty miles outside of Clearview and the road was empty. Just like the road into the wilderness would be. Except for the trucks. They'd be driving that road, the cold gray sky hanging over them, the dark forest pressing in on them, and the pockmarked road stretching out in front of them. I'd be the only other person on that road.

I blunted this line of thinking before it took over. I focused on the here and now. I looked down to the shoreline below the road. The waves were breaking hard. The ocean was angry, and that was fine with me. I liked the ocean regardless of its mood. It reminded me of my dad. We used to walk along that shoreline and he'd tell me how the world worked. He knew because he knew science. Others didn't.

"THE WORLD IS made up of four elements," my dad had said. "Air, Fire, Water and Earth."

Of course, he knew that these weren't the real elements, but I was only four at the time and he was laying the groundwork for something else. For a secret he wanted to tell me. The biggest secret in the world.

We both looked out over the ocean. The sun was red orange, the ocean dark blue, and the waves broke white and big.

My dad said, "Water is the most important element."

I thought he'd said that because we lived in Clearview, a water town. But that wasn't the reason. The reason was that groundwork. He wanted me to understand a few basics first. Then he'd tell me the secret.

But he never did tell me. Not on that day or any other day. Before he could, the marauders murdered him.

I LOOKED BACK up from the ocean and the massive plant came into view. It was a grand structure, but it was old. Its iron beams were coated in thick, brown rust and its concrete walls were gouged from the battering of ocean storms.

I pulled into the parking lot. One third full. The night shift was still on, and the morning shift, my shift, wouldn't pull in for another two hours.

I walked toward the plant's entrance and glanced

up at the faded green letters above the doors. I wondered if this was the last time I'd see them. They spelled out the name of the company that used to own the plant, 'Corolaqua.' But Corolaqua, like all companies, and all states and countries, was long gone.

MANY DECADES AGO, the Passim Virus killed almost everyone. The few who'd survived it lived in small towns along the west coast, and they fended for themselves. They hunted and fished and grew their own food.

Then, as things stabilized, the small towns started trading with each other. First food, then machines. Computers, refrigerators, washers and dryers, and every piece of equipment that still worked. They called them Remnants, and the more they broke down, the more valuable the ones that still worked became. So valuable that people risked their lives salvaging them from the dead cities where the Passim Virus still lurked.

A few small towns were luckier than others. They could still produce fresh water (like Clearview) or fuel or electricity. Every town needed water, fuel, and electricity, so these towns traded for the best food and the best Remnants.

And the truck towns did fine, too. They supplied the trucks that kept the whole show going. Without trucks, there wouldn't be any trading, and without trading, there wouldn't be any Territory. (The Territory was the unofficial name for this nameless affiliation of towns.)

I STEPPED INTO the control room and saw Joe McDonough and Green Haily stationed up front, staring at the bank of monitors. They both glanced at me without bothering to hide their contempt. No big deal. I was used to it.

In the back, Frank Bannon, the plant foreman, was sitting at his desk. He launched right in, "It's about two hundred miles south."

"What's it running at?" I asked.

"About seventy-five percent." He handed me the paperwork: A visa with the Clearview seal on it, directions for the trip south, instructions on how to repair the pump, and a list of the supplies I'd need for the job.

I looked up from the paperwork and caught a flash of regret on Frank's face. Frank was a good guy and he felt bad for sending me out. He knew it was a death sentence. But it wasn't his choice. The last hire was always the first to go and that policy made sense. The man with the least experience was expendable. If the marauders murdered him or if the Virus killed him, it wouldn't be that big a loss.

But Frank knew that in my case, this policy didn't make sense. If equipment right here at the plant broke down, a far greater problem than a malfunction in the far reaches of the Territory, I'd be the only one with a shot at fixing it. The other workers at the plant knew how to operate the equipment assigned to them and could perform minor repairs, but they couldn't fix a major breakdown. They didn't even understand how each piece of equipment worked in conjunction with the others to purify seawater.

The intake valves under the shoreline inhaled the seawater into the plant. The water then traveled through gigantic, high-density plastic pipes, where dosing pumps adjusted the flow rate. (My job at the plant was to operate one of those dosing pumps.) The water then spiraled through huge gravity filters and reverse osmosis cells and when it came out of those cells, it was ready for the Territory.

If you knew the chemistry and physics behind the process, it really wasn't too hard to follow. But even McDonough and Haily, who monitored the whole process for the morning shift, didn't understand it. They were trained to read the monitors, spot signs of trouble, and report that trouble to Frank. I gave Frank credit. He understood the process as well as you could without knowing the science behind it.

"After you load up the van, go home and pick up whatever you're gonna need," he said. "If it's just a damn animal that crawled in there, you'll be back to-morrow. But if it's a big job, count on three days."

I LOADED UP the Corolaqua van, left my car in the parking lot, and headed back to my place. It'd been three years since the last pump broke down. Back then, Frank had sent Gary Ledic out to fix it and that was the last anyone saw of him. Some people said marauders had killed him, but most thought it'd been the Virus.

The Virus lived everywhere. My dad had taught me that it was originally called the Passim Virus because 'passim' meant 'everywhere' in Latin. I'd since learned that 'passim' meant more than 'everywhere.' It meant 'scattered around randomly' and that was the perfect description. The Virus still lived in dead cities. In Seat-tle, Portland, San Francisco, Los Angeles, San Diego, and every city in between. And it lived in the wilder-ness. That's why people never left their towns. That, and the marauders.

As for myself, I didn't care whether the marauders had killed Ledic or the Virus had or that he'd been killed at all. I didn't like him. He'd tried to murder me. So when he didn't come back, it was one less thing for me to think about.

Chapter Two

AT HOME, I packed for the trip south. My dad used to go on trips but they weren't suicide missions like this one. Town Councils would hire him when a crucial piece of machinery in their towns broke down. My dad knew science, so sometimes he could fix the machinery. There weren't many around like him. Now there were even less. Way less.

The day before he'd go on a trip, he'd fry us fish and potatoes for dinner. In the late afternoons, we'd drive out to Hickemy's and we'd pick out the fillets. That was our ritual. But the day before he left for Merryville, the last day I ever saw him, he changed our ritual.

We still headed to Hickemy's, but this time we stopped at the beach first. We never walked the shoreline the day before his trips. And he didn't launch into whatever he was going to teach me like he usually did on these walks. He was silent. *And* his breathing was faster than normal.

The red orange sun was sliding into the sea, and some of the white caps were big while others were small. The ocean couldn't decide whether to be calm or anxious, just like my dad.

We sat on the sand and watched the sun turn deep red. The white caps danced. My dad put his arm around my shoulders and I waited for him to talk, to tell me why we hadn't gone straight to Hickemy's. Instead, he told me that there was the same amount of water on Earth right now as there'd been millions of years ago. He said that Earth never lost nor gained water.

That seemed impossible and I didn't believe him.

He said that water went round and round. Evaporating, condensing, raining, and evaporating again. He went into detail about the sun's heat, transpiration, and cool air and clouds.

But I was thinking about Jimmy Hickemy, the fisherman.

Every dawn, Jimmy sailed his boat out to sea and fished until noon. Every afternoon, in his back yard, he gutted, cleaned and filleted his catch. Every evening, on his back porch, he'd lay the fish out on beds of shiny ice, and people from Clearview would come by and pick up their dinner.

"The world is a big place," my dad said.

I looked at the ocean. He was right. I couldn't see where the world ended.

"But it's mostly water," he said, and looked up to the sky. "That's what you see when you look down from the stars."

I looked up to the sky. "I know," I said, and I did. He'd already taught me that there were stars and planets out there. Galaxies and solar systems. Thousands of them. He'd taught me that a vast majority of those planets didn't have water. Earth was special because it had water.

"Never stop learning, Roy," he said, then kissed the top of my head.

"I won't, Dad."

WE PULLED UP to Jimmy Hickemy's dilapidated ranch house. There were a few cars and a bunch of bicycles out front.

I hurried into the back yard and up the steps onto the porch. I squeezed between customers picking out fillets and started to check out the fish. White, pink, and orange fillets, neatly laid out over ice.

Jimmy saw me. "What'll it be?" he said. He always treated me like an adult and I liked it.

I looked at the halibut. That's what I wanted.

"Let's see what your dad says," Jimmy said.

I expected my dad to say 'no.' We hadn't bought Halibut in a while. It was more expensive than the other fillets.

My dad made it up to the porch and saw that I was standing in front of the Halibut.

"Please, dad," I said.

He looked over the fillets. "They look pretty good, don't they?"

"Good enough to eat," I said.

He laughed, and Jimmy laughed, too.

"Give us a couple of good ones, Jimmy," my dad said. "Good enough to eat."

I laughed.

MY DAD AND I sliced the potatoes. I did it carefully, like he'd taught me. When we finished, he put the slices into the pan and as soon as they hit the oil, the kitchen filled with sizzling.

He was quiet, concentrating on the cooking. More so than usual. The silence made the popping and crackling of the oil louder than I'd ever heard it.

He battered the fish and began to fry it in the black

iron skillet. He glanced at me a couple of times and smiled.

I watched him standing in front of the stove, cooking us dinner. I loved him.

I PACKED ENOUGH food for four days and also packed a bottle of Curado. Curado was the rarest, most expensive alcohol in the Territory. It'd been distilled in Nahcotta, a town up north in what used to be Washington State. Nahcotta was the last town to have an industrial distillery that worked. It'd stopped working thirty years ago.

Someone had given my dad three bottles of the fabled liquor for a job he'd done. My dad had slowly sipped through one bottle, but two remained. He wasn't a drinker.

After I finished packing a couple changes of clothes, I started to pick out a book for the trip. If I ended up spending a few nights in the wilderness, I wanted to be prepared. I always read before bed. My dad had read to me every night and I'd kept the tradition up. The house was full of books. His books. And he'd always taken a book on his trips.

I REMEMBERED WATCHING him going through the rows of books for his last trip. The fish and potatoes from dinner were still warm in my stomach.

"Air?" he asked.

"East," I said.

"Water?" he said.

"West."

"Fire?"

"South."

"Earth?"

"North."

I was nine years old and my father had taught me the real elements and the periodic table, but we still had fun with the original four. Ancient civilizations, the ones that had believed in these elements, associated each of them with a direction and with certain animals.

"Air is eagle and falcon," I said, "Water is dolphin and turtle. Earth is bull and bear. And Fire is lion and—," I paused before delivering the punch line, "— salamander."

He laughed at salamander. It was a running joke between us. In one of my dad's books, we'd read that one ancient civilization had grouped salamanders with Fire. But salamanders were amphibians and we wondered why they hadn't been grouped with water. So I'd said, "Fire stole salamanders from Water and headed south." (South was Fire's direction.)

My dad liked that theory and we ended up building a whole mythology around it. All the animals had originally flocked to Water because it was the most important element. So the other elements became jealous and started stealing Water's animals. We'd spend hours weaving stories about the sneaky ways that Air, Fire, and Earth stole animals from Water.

My dad finally pulled a book down from one of the shelves and I saw the title. *The Old Man and the Sea.* (It'd be years before I realized that he meant for me to see that title and to understand that it was connected to the secret.)

The next morning, before he left for Merryville, he drove me to school. He told me that after school I was to go home with Rick Levingworth. I'd spend the night there and he'd pick me up from school the next afternoon.

I went to school, spent the night at the Levingworth's, but the next day, after school, my dad didn't pick me up. I waited until everyone was gone before I accepted Mrs. Levingworth's offer to drive me home. We got to my house, but my dad wasn't there either. So Mrs. Levingworth said I'd go home with her and wait there, and we'd check back later.

But I didn't want to go and she caved in. We stayed.

Rick and I played a game on a computer that my dad had rebuilt. In the game, alien ships attacked us and we tried to shoot them down. Very few families in town had computers that worked, and almost none had computer games, so Rick was happy to hang out at my house.

I started getting worried when I noticed Mrs. Levingworth hovering near the phone. It looked like she wanted to make a phone call. But my dad didn't work with anyone, so I wasn't sure who she was planning to call. Maybe the police. Clearview had two policemen.

When evening fell, Mrs. Levingworth's worry was palpable. She told me it was time to go to her house. I'd spend the night there. She said that my dad was spending the night in Merryville. But she hadn't made any phone calls so I wondered how she'd found that out. She couldn't know that.

I wanted to wait for my dad and I stationed myself at the front window.

She tried to coax me into going home with her and Rick. It was dinnertime and she wanted to cook us dinner.

I said I wanted to stay and wait. I wouldn't leave. So she finally went ahead and made some calls. I didn't know it at the time, but she asked the police to check in with the Fibs. The Fibs were in charge of policing the Territory. When there was a serious problem, towns would call them in.

Then Mrs. Levingworth made dinner, and I ate my dinner in front of the window.

Mrs. Levingworth told me everything would be okay. She repeated that my dad was spending the night in Merryville.

I DIDN'T GO to bed that night. I stared out the window. Rick and Mrs. Levingworth spent the night at my house.

I watched the night get darker.

I watched the dawn rise. A haunting purple sky.

I waited for my dad.

Mrs. Levingworth made breakfast.

I didn't eat.

Then it was time to go to school, but I didn't want to go to school.

Mrs. Levingworth called Mrs. Simmons and had her swing by and take Rick to school. Mrs. Levingworth stayed with me, but we didn't talk.

I waited.

Sometime around noon, a car pulled up to the house and Mr. Kadish stepped out. I saw him hesitate before approaching the house.

He came to the door and I don't know if Mrs. Levingworth heard his car, but she opened the door before he knocked. He stepped inside and saw me by the window. He smiled, but it wasn't a smile. It was something sad that looked like a smile.

He and Mrs. Levingworth headed into the kitchen

without talking.

I moved quietly toward the kitchen door to listen. They spoke in somber tones and I couldn't make out the words, but I could tell they were sad words.

I went back to the window and stared outside.

Mrs. Levingworth walked out of the kitchen. Mr. Kadish followed. He headed to the front door and left.

Mrs. Levingworth stepped up to me and said we needed to talk.

I said, "Let's wait until my dad comes home."

Another hour passed before she was ready to talk and I was ready to listen.

She told me that my dad had died. She didn't tell me how or why and I didn't ask. That would come later.

I saw tears roll down her face and I saw her lips quiver.

She hugged me tight and I felt her body trembling.

I was alone.

Chapter Three

I DROVE THE Corolaqua van to Troy Street. I wanted to say good-bye to Benny before heading out.

All that made Clearview a town, except for its most important asset, Corolaqua, was on Troy Street. The shops that sold food, clothes, and Remnants, and the few repair and trade shops that weren't run out of people's houses. The Town Hall was also here. Like every other town in the Territory, a Town Council ran Clearview and six days a week, the Councilmen showed up at the Town Hall and did their best to keep Clearview functional. The Town Hall also housed the Line, which was how all the towns communicated with each other. The Line held the Territory together. Barely.

Benny ran the Line in Clearview.

I MET BENNY Spokane in kindergarten. Back then, I had other friends, too, because kids didn't resent me yet. They liked that I knew things, and they asked me questions about those things and I answered them.

Benny was one of the kids who asked me questions. His family, like all families, didn't encourage him to learn more than what he was taught in school. So when Benny found out that there was a lot more to learn, he turned to me. Before the Virus, schools taught all sorts of subjects, but now they stuck to the basics. Enough to communicate and survive in a world of rudimentary living. And parents could stop sending their kids to school whenever they wanted to. It was more important for your kid to help grow food or sew shirts or fish or chop wood or keep an old car or bicycle going. Or to work one of the necessary jobs in town.

In third grade, after my dad was murdered, kids stopped asking me questions. They were scared of me, like I was tainted by my dad's death. Benny stopped asking me questions, too. But he didn't have that same look in his eyes that the other kids had. When I'd catch other kids staring at me, their eyes were full of fear. Benny's eyes were full of questions.

Finally, after a couple of months, he was so desperate to learn new things that he couldn't hold out any longer. He started asking me questions again. I answered the ones I could and if I didn't know the answer, I was so happy to have someone ask questions again, that I'd go home and look it up.

I was living with the Levingworths. They took me in after my dad was murdered. But every weekend, they'd let me go back to my house for a few hours and I took advantage of that. I'd look through my dad's books and find answers to Benny's questions, and that led me back to my dad. I was keeping my promise to him. That I'd always keep learning. And this sealed my friendship with Benny.

By fifth grade, Benny didn't have to ask me questions anymore. I'd voluntarily tell him what I was learning. And by seventh grade, Benny was returning the favor. He was learning things on his own and teaching them to me. He didn't have the resources I had, my father's books, CDs, DVDs, old flash drives crammed with information, etc. Instead, he'd sneak into Clearview's abandoned buildings and dig up old books and magazines. He'd even sneak into the school's old warehouse on Edgerton and spend hours there, reading study guides the teachers had long ago abandoned.

By eighth grade, most of the other kids were ostracizing us. And in ninth grade, they began to kick the crap out of us. Benny was small so he was an easy target. Kids would beat him up anywhere, anytime. But he got used to it and did a good job of hiding the purple bruises the punches left. He knew that snitching would make things worse.

I was a big kid, so kids had to plan their attacks on me and make sure they outnumbered me. They'd ambush me with overwhelming force and even though I'd fight back, I'd take a pounding. I could fight one or two kids, but three or more was too much. Still, sometimes I'd get in some good punches. Like Benny, I hid the bruises, but Mrs. Levingworth still figured it out and talked to the parents of the guilty kids. She was protective of me because I had no one but her, but it made things worse and I had to tell her to stop.

There were two other smart kids in our school, Rick Levingworth (who got stuck with me as his 'foster' brother, more on that later) and Ellen Sanchez, and maybe you could say they were smarter than me because they chose to play dumb and fit in. (Only later, did they feel it was okay to exercise some of their smarts.) No one in town was sympathetic to smart kids or to smart adults. And it wasn't really being 'smart' that was the problem. It was that no one believed learning facts, concepts, theories, or subjects which had long been forgotten could help their town survive.

At that age, I thought that this was just the way it was. But as I grew older, I began to wonder *why* it was this way. It'd be years before I learned the answer.

First, I'd have to discover that secret my dad had wanted to tell me.

I STEPPED INTO the Town Hall and the building was quiet. No one was in this early, except for Benny. Benny's 'office' was in the basement and that was fine with him. The Councilmen were too lazy to head down there, so they didn't bother him much.

I headed down the stairs and to the end of the hallway and knocked on Benny's door. No answer. But I was sure he was in there working on computer code and entranced by it. I opened the door and stepped into a small room packed with computer monitors, hard drives, assorted hardware, and a mass of cables. Some of the hardware was dedicated to the Line, but most of it was Benny's personal stash. He'd rebuilt these Remnants himself.

Benny was sitting in front of a monitor, scrolling through lines of code. He was small and wiry and his leg jittered when he was anxious. If he was concentrating on computer code, his leg never jittered.

"Got a problem with the exec files?" he said, without looking up from his work.

"Nope."

"Then why the visit?" He didn't want to be bothered. Nothing was happening on the Line so this was a good time for him to work on his own stuff.

"Take a guess," I said.

He stopped checking code and looked at me and I didn't have to say it. He knew. His leg started jittering.

"Sending you out is just plain dumb," he said, "a losing strategy. Frank knows that."

"He's gotta follow the rules," I said.

"Not in this case."

"They'd turn on him in two seconds if he sent someone else," I said, and that was the truth. The plant workers would vote in a new foreman by the end of the day if Frank gave me special treatment. "If you don't come back, the plant's over," Benny said.

"The plant did fine before me. It'll do fine after."

"We both know that's a bunch of crap."

Benny was right. But only partially. He was right that I was the only one who had a shot at fixing a serious breakdown, but it was also a fact that the plant had never had a serious breakdown. The truth was, that way before I came along, someone always managed to find a way to make the necessary repairs. Why water plants, refineries, and electric plants continued to function was a mystery. A lucky mystery that no one questioned. They didn't know enough to question it.

"What are you hearing?" I said. I wanted to know what kind of danger I was heading into, and the Line was the only source for that.

"Bandon said they lost a trucker a couple days ago," Benny said. "A marauder attack." Bandon was a truck town.

"What about the Virus?" I asked.

"Three cases yesterday. Four the day before."

"Not bad."

"Tell that to the deceased," he said, and glanced up at me. "Just don't do any exploring."

"I'm sticking to the road and the pumping station."

It wasn't that long ago that Benny and I used to talk about exploring the Territory. We were sure that there was a bonanza of knowledge hidden out there and we wanted to find it. But the reality was that we'd given

up on ever venturing out of Clearview. The chance of
dying from the Virus or at the hands of the marauders
was just too great. Not to mention that leaving Clearview without a visa was desertion and the Fibs jailed
all deserters. Though we never actually said it, we were
too frightened to leave. Our fears were greater than our
dreams.

"Maybe when I get back, you'll have figured out
what those data packets are," I said.

"Don't count on it. It's too weird a code."

Over the last two years, Benny had noticed mysterious data packets moving through the Line. At first,
he'd thought a fellow Lineman from another town was
behind them. But after digging around a little, he'd
concluded that none of the other Linemen knew
enough to pull this off. Like everyone else in the Territory, they knew how to do their jobs, but that was it.
They didn't even know that the Line was a stripped
down version of an expansive communications network once called the Internet. Before the Virus, all
kinds of information had flowed through this network.
Even video. Back then, bandwidth was big enough to
carry a ton of information. Bandwidth was like the
pipes and aqueducts that carried water from Corolaqua
to other towns. But while Corolaqua's pipes and aqueducts could still carry plenty of water, what was left of
the Internet was barely enough bandwidth to connect
the towns.

"Any sign of trouble," Benny said, "and you run as
fast you can." Then he suddenly stood up and hugged
me. It was a rare emotional display of our friendship,
and what it meant was obvious. He knew I might not
return.

Chapter Four

I HEADED SOUTH. To my right, rugged gray cliffs ran down to the ocean. To my left, a dark green forest ran inland as far as the eye could see. The road was worn and for long stretches, the lane lines were gone. Then, out of nowhere, I'd see a few, patchy and faded, like mysterious hieroglyphics from an ancient culture.

Decent roads meant trucks could haul goods up and down the Territory, so some towns used road repair to trade for goods. Percy, a mid-size town, took care of this stretch of road, but I was sure that lane lines were its last priority. Over the last couple of years, five men from Percy had died from the Virus. They'd caught it while working on the roads, but every town did what it could to survive.

The road soon veered away from the ocean and deeper into the wilderness, an endless forest of lime green, black green, and hues of green I'd never seen before. I wanted to see trucks on the road, but I didn't and that made me wary. Everyone in the Territory knew the wilderness was home to the marauders. They'd found pockets of land without the Virus and these sanctuaries became the base camps from which they'd ambush truckers and workers on the roads.

I kept my eyes on the forest looking for signs of an ambush and stayed hyper-alert for the next three hours until the road veered back toward the ocean. As soon as I saw the blue Pacific, I felt safer and calmer. I knew a lot about the ocean and about water.

A FEW YEARS after the marauders murdered my father, I began to teach myself as much as I could about water. I had decided that the time had come to find out why my father had impressed on me that water was important.

I studied the science books which he'd salvaged, and I verified what he'd said on the beach that day: There was a finite amount of water on Earth. Earth never gained nor lost water. I learned the water cycle in detail, going way beyond what my dad had taught me. I learned about oceans, rivers, streams, lakes, glaciers and underground aquifers. I learned that humans, themselves, were seventy percent water. Then I taught myself exactly how the Corolaqua plant purified seawater and I studied the chemistry of water, a compound, not an element, made of hydrogen and oxygen, which *were* elements. I continued on with chemistry, then biology and physics. I was building on the foundation that my father had laid down.

But I went too far. At least, according to everyone in Clearview. They thought I was obsessed with useless knowledge, and they thought it was because I didn't want to face losing my dad. They said that I was obsessed with learning because I was trying to fill a hole in my life. A bottomless hole that could never be filled. To everyone in town, I was crazy. Psychologically damaged beyond repair.

So, as I got older, I decided to keep what I knew to myself and I made more of an effort to fit in, like Rick Levingworth and Ellen Sanchez did. It took a while, but it worked. Most people stopped thinking I was crazy. Unfortunately, they instead started to think I looked down on them and started to resent me again. Still, that was better than it'd been and it would've been a good way to leave it, but I made things worse. I discovered that there was something going on with the water.

A FEW YEARS out of school, I decided to compile a kind of almanac about the Territory. The number of towns, their populations, the amount and kind of food they produced, the goods and services they provided, how much they traded, etc. I wanted to gather together as many facts about each town as I could.

But information was hard to come by. Much harder than I'd expected. So I enlisted Benny's help. He tried to verify information through the Line. But the people who ran the Line in other towns were suspicious. Answering these questions wasn't part of their jobs. The Line was for trade, reports about the Virus and marauders, and communication between the towns and the Fibs. Most of his requests never received answers at all, like they'd completely disappeared from the Line.

At first, my plan was to build an accurate portrait of the Territory, but that soon changed into something else. I started crunching numbers and then I took those numbers and referenced them to what I knew about Corolaqua's water output. That's when I began to see that things didn't add up.

Under any possible scenario, Corolaqua was pumping out way more water than needed. Corolaqua provided water for the towns from Port Orford to Astoria, and those towns' populations couldn't possibly consume all the water we pumped out. And the desalination plant in Willapa Bay, which served the towns north of Astoria up to Moclips, wasn't needed at all. Between what we pumped out and the rainfall and aquifers up there, they had plenty of water.

Then, by carefully tracking trade on the Line, Benny and I suspected the same thing was going on in the southern part of the Territory. We couldn't confirm it, but it looked like there were three desalination plants south of Port Orford, in what used to be California. But the towns down there required only one plant, if any. There just weren't enough people in the Territory to justify five plants operating at full capacity. Way more water was being purified and shipped than needed, including water required for farming. No matter how you added it up, the numbers didn't make any sense.

So where was all this extra water going? Was it being shipped inland? But there were no towns inland. At least that's what we'd been taught all our lives. It was rumored that there might be a string of towns on the east coast, but no one had ever confirmed that. And even if that were true, it didn't make sense that water was being purified on one coast and trucked across two thousand miles of dead land to the other coast. Was it possible that some towns in the Territory were using the water for something that the rest of us didn't know about? I didn't have an answer to that question, but I became obsessed with finding one.

I should've kept my discovery to myself because, when I brought it up to others, I was branded a troublemaker. Clearview considered itself lucky to be a supplier of water. Water was a precious commodity. Why ask questions about it?

And late at night, when I was lying in bed, I'd stare up at the ceiling and wonder if everyone else was right and I was wrong. Was I psychologically damaged? Was I obsessed with water because of my father? He'd said that water was important and now I'd found out

that there was something weird going on with it. A secret? Or was I just trying to keep him alive? I wanted
him alive. I missed him.

Chapter Five

I HADN'T PASSED any trucks. The road had been empty the entire way. The only sign of life had been the white seagulls skimming the gray blue ocean.

I entered the Swan Peninsula and focused more closely on my surroundings. The pumping station would be somewhere just up ahead. My simple map didn't show the exact location, but it'd be easy to find. Here, the aqueduct channel ran inland parallel to the road and about a quarter mile to the east of it. And I knew that pumping stations were installed where water had to run uphill. Otherwise, gravity did the job of pulling water through the aqueducts.

So I started to look for a rise in the terrain. The pumping station would be where that rise began.

COROLAQUA'S WATER DISTRIBUTION system wasn't complicated. The plant delivered its water through open channel aqueducts, covered aqueducts, and pipes directly to reservoirs up and down the coast. Towns used the water from those reservoirs for themselves or they shipped it in tank trucks to towns not served by the reservoirs.

Once in a while, the flow of water would stop. A pipe would break or a tree branch would crash into an open channel or, as now, a pumping station would fail. Whatever the problem was, Corolaqua would have to send a worker out to fix it.

TEN MINUTES INTO the Swan Peninsula, I saw the treetops rising, which meant that just to my east, I'd find the pumping station. So I swung across the road and pulled over onto the shoulder. The shoulder was covered in vegetation which had grown out from the woods. I looked into the dense forest and every shade of green stared back at me.

I didn't unload any tools. I'd check the pumping station first, find out what the problem was, then return with the right tools. For now, a gas lantern to light up the inside of the pumping station would be enough. I also didn't take any protective gear. Over the decades, such gear had proved useless against the Virus. Even the few Remnant biohazard suits that had been salvaged over the years didn't do any good. That fact alone should've clued people in that something didn't make scientific sense about the Virus, but, again, no one knew enough to get that.

I HIKED THROUGH the thick woods, leaving the warmth and light of the road behind. The Western Hemlocks' thick canopy blocked out so much sunlight that it left the underbrush starved and thin. I was surrounded by a cold, damp darkness and that meant marauders, so I tuned in to the sounds around me. I heard birds chirping, small animals skittering, and branches rustling. Sounds I'd heard before. They weren't ominous sounds, but without human sounds to engulf them, they were harshly exaggerated. (The Virus had killed humans but spared animals and no one knew why. But at least, this made scientific sense. There had been other viruses with that characteristic.)

After fifteen minutes or so, I heard the soft rush of

water and saw sunlight up ahead. Twenty-five yards later, I stepped into an open swath of land that cut a path right through the woods. A concrete channel, carrying water, ran down the center of the path, and there was enough sunlight here to spur the undergrowth to life. The vegetation was so vibrant that it used the metal mesh that covered the channel as a trellis and crept all the way across the aqueduct.

I looked to my south and, two hundred yards down, I saw the pumping station. It was a concrete and wood enclosure about the size of a small room. The channel fed into it and I could see that the water was backed up.

As I approached the pumping station, I heard the spasmodic rhythm of the pumps inside. That ragged tempo meant that there was probably something wrong with the pumps, rather than the machinery that drove them. The machinery was trying to do its job, but something was stopping one or more of the pumps from following through.

I opened the door to the pumping station, stepped inside, lit the gas lantern, and immediately saw that someone had smashed one of the four pumps. The plastic cylinder which housed the pump had been cracked wide open and, inside, the pump was bent, but still moving, sporadically. Luckily, each pump was controlled by its own machinery, so the other three were fine.

My immediate thought was *marauders*. But my next thought was *why*? Why would they sabotage the distribution of water? Stealing water made sense, but why sabotage the flow? To punish a town downstream? But if they wanted to do that, they would've smashed all the pumps. Maybe it wasn't marauders.

I spend the next couple hours checking the machinery for each pump. It all worked. Then I headed back toward the van, keeping an eye out for marauders the entire way.

I picked up the supplies I'd need for the repairs and returned. Then I made another trip for tools. I still hadn't seen any marauders, but on that third trip back, I felt like I was being watched. I caught glimpses of squirrels, raccoons, and a large deer so I told myself that they were the ones watching me.

I worked late into the evening and then called it a day. It was going to take me another twelve hours to finish, so I'd get up early tomorrow and start again then.

I set up a small tent nearby, built a small fire and ate a light meal. Even though I'd worked hard, I wasn't that hungry because I was anxious. I still felt like I was being watched. After eating, I pulled out the book I'd brought, *Ender's Game*, and read by the fire.

I FIRST READ *Ender's Game* when I was six. My dad had said that I'd love it, but I didn't. He liked science fiction and rated *Ender's Game* one of his top five sci-fi books. At the time, I thought, what's the big deal? A kid saves the world. I'd already read books with that plot and I didn't find the specifics anything special. Ender's world was boring. It was a hyped-up version of school.

A few years later, after my dad was gone, I read it again and this time I loved it. I understood it. The book wasn't about Ender's world. It was about Ender. His classmates hated him, picked on him, and beat the crap out of him, all because he was different. Like I was. I wasn't brilliant like Ender, not even close, and I never rose to the top either, but my classmates did hate me and kick the crap out of me. And like Ender, I fought back even when I was outnumbered. Back then, I'd wondered if my dad wanted me to read this book because he knew that some day I'd identify with Ender, a boy who had few friends.

I still wonder about that.

I read until the fire died, the entire time planning to open that bottle of Curado. I wasn't a drinker, but a drink would've been a good defense against the dark. I never opened the bottle.

Before heading into my tent, I looked up at the sky and saw a thin crescent moon between the branches of the hemlocks. It offered almost no light. I maneuvered so I could get a better look at the sky, hoping to catch a glimpse of a shooting star. My dad had paid close attention to shooting stars. He'd said that, before the Virus, people couldn't see many stars. The ambient light created by thousands of cities had made star gazing almost impossible. But now the stars shone bright, millions of gold specks lighting up the night sky, a consolation prize courtesy of the Virus. And the shooting stars were the brightest of all.

I knew they weren't really stars, but meteors entering the earth's atmosphere and burning up. But on that cold dark night, I had no idea that they were also part of a bigger connection between my life and Ender's life.

I couldn't get a clear angle on the sky, so I crawled into my tent, slid into my sleeping bag, and tried to fall asleep.

Chapter Six

THE NIGHT SOUNDS were louder than I'd expected. Louder than the water rushing through the channel and louder than the rhythmic beating of the three working pumps. The night was dominated by the hoots of owls, the symphony of chirping crickets, and the scurrying of mice and raccoons and every so often, the deer added their human-like snorts to the blanket of sounds.

I don't know how long it took me to fall asleep, but I do know that I awoke abruptly. *Someone was out there.* I don't know how I knew, it could've been the subtle change in the sea of night sounds, but I knew. And I was guessing it was a marauder.

I reached over and grabbed the bowie knife I'd brought with me and I suddenly wished I'd made the effort to acquire a gun. Guns were illegal Remnants, and expensive, and only Fibs were allowed to own them.

I slid out of my sleeping bag, crouched low in my tent, and tried to pick out more hints of the marauder. The cadence of scurrying mice and raccoons had changed and so had the pitch of the owls' hoots.

Then I heard silence take over the space behind my tent and I pictured the marauder standing there, ready to attack.

I crouched, motionless, and realized that my heart was pumping wildly.

I had a couple of choices. I could race out of my

tent, across the top of the channel, hopefully light-stepping it enough so I wouldn't fall through the metal mesh, and disappear into the woods on the other side. Or I could charge the marauder with my bowie knife. But if he were armed, he'd shoot me. Of course, he could do that even if I high-tailed it across the channel. So I stayed stock-still and tried to come up with another plan.

The silence behind my tent started to fill back up with night sounds. The marauder must've been circling around to the front, but I couldn't hear his footsteps.

I made a decision right then.

I scooped up the keys to my van, stuffed it in my pocket, unzipped the tent flap as fast as I could and sprang out of the tent. I raced back around, into the woods, gaining speed with every step, running as fast as I could toward the road. I didn't look back for the marauder.

I ran, stumbled and regained my balance, and repeated that over and over again, lurching forward in the dark, adrenaline and fear propelling me. I avoided tree trunks as best I could and ignored the scrapes and cuts accumulating on my bare feet and arms. I lost my bowie knife somewhere along the way.

I finally saw the road up ahead and scanned the shoulder for my van. Only then did I consider that another marauder might be stationed out here. I buried that thought and exploded out of the woods, pulling the keys from my pocket. I spotted my van, and it was clear of marauders.

I ran to it, unlocked the door, jumped in, jammed the keys into the ignition and as the engine roared to life, one word crossed my mind.

Coward.

I was a coward, running from the marauders. The marauders who murdered my father and destroyed my life.

I turned on the headlights, put the van in gear, and was just about to hit the gas, when I saw him. He was standing in front of the van and, if I pressed the gas, I'd barrel right into him, killing him.

I hesitated.

The man wasn't holding a weapon and his arms were down by his sides. His eyes were fixed on me but I knew that he couldn't really see me in the glare of the headlights. So I took a second to look him over.

He was a big man, tall and unyielding. And he looked old, but rugged, like old age had made him stronger, not weaker. The skin on his face was weathered like dark armor, proud and invincible.

But why was he standing in front of my van, in the dead of night, with no weapon?

I didn't put my foot on the gas.

He approached the van.

I didn't move. Was it possible that he wasn't a marauder?

I watched him walk up to my door. He stopped a couple of yards away and didn't make another move. I waited a few seconds, then stepped outside.

He glanced at my hands and saw that I wasn't holding a weapon.

"You're right about the water," he said. His voice was calm and as still as the night.

My mind reeled. How did he know about my discovery? Did he know who I was?

"I can't answer all your questions," he said. "Right now, it's too dangerous to talk. My name is Jim Crater—"

Suddenly, to my right, I saw a shooting star streak across the vast black sky. He looked over and saw it, too, its gold tail shimmering.

"That's not a star," he said and then looked back at me. "Don't stop here. Keep moving south."

And then he walked away, down the road.

I watched him until he disappeared into the dark and then realized, I hadn't said a word.

Chapter Seven

BACK IN MY tent, I analyzed what Jim Crater had said.

He could've learned from anyone in Clearview that I was the nut with the crazy theory about the water. Or from a trucker passing through. But he'd said *you're right about the water* and that was jarring. He was saying that excess water *was* being shipped throughout the Territory. Or, at the very least, it meant that *he* believed that. So *why* did he believe that?

And why did he say that the shooting star hadn't been a star? Did he know it was a meteor entering the earth's atmosphere? Did he know science? And I couldn't figure out why he'd tracked me down to say so little. Why didn't he just tell me exactly why he'd cornered me?

And finally, why did he want me to keep moving south?

I thought all these questions through and I probably wouldn't have been able to stop thinking them through, which would've kept me up all night, if the long day's work hadn't finally caught up to me. I fell asleep right away with only one issue resolved. I wasn't going to take Jim Crater's advice. I wasn't going to keep moving south. I'd finish my job and head north, back to Clearview.

A FEW HOURS later, dawn rose and lit up the forest, and I geared up for the day. I planned to work as hard as I could so I'd be able to head back home tonight. But as soon as I stepped out of my tent, my eyes fell on something that threatened to change that plan.

I saw a sketch in the dirt. It was crude, but I could tell what it was. A reptilian body with four squat legs, a long thick tail, a broad snout, and protruding eyes.

It was a salamander.

And above it, I saw twigs laid out in the form of an arrow. The arrow pointed from the salamander to the charred wood from last night's fire.

The element was Fire.

The animal was a salamander.

The direction was south.

Fire stole salamanders from Water and headed south. That connection was engrained in me from childhood. Engrained right alongside the memory of my father. It was part of my father.

Maybe the animal wasn't a salamander. Maybe it was an iguana or a gecko or a chameleon. But it wasn't. It was a salamander.

Fire stole salamanders from Water and headed south.

Crater had drawn the salamander to reiterate his message from last night. *Keep moving south.*

But how did he know about the ancient elements? That each had their own animals? That each had their own *direction*? Had he learned that as a child, like I had? But how did he know that *I* knew about them? How did he know that *for me*, drawing a salamander would turn Fire into south? And that question led to the most disturbing question of all.

Did Crater know my father?

I DIDN'T STOP to think more about that question, but went right to work. As I was repairing the pump, all the questions from the prior night ran through my mind. But I couldn't come up with any answers. I didn't have enough information.

By late morning, I'd decided that the only question I had to answer was whether to head south or back to Clearview. Even though I'd already dismissed heading south, it now seemed like the only way to get some answers.

The repairs went smoothly and the hours passed quickly. At three, I took a break to eat. I sat by the pumping station, staring south, where the wilderness rose to a peak, and that's when an answer to one of those earlier questions took shape. I understood why someone had sabotaged the pumping station. They wanted to draw a Corolaqua worker out here. The next man on the list. The man with the theory about the water.

I was sure that Crater had waited on that peak in the distance, waited until he saw me arrive, then, in the dead of night, he had hiked down to deliver his message. *Keep moving south.* And he'd added such a compelling illustration to his message, that he knew I'd take it seriously.

JUST BEFORE EVENING, I finished. Then I cleaned up the pumping station, checked again to see that everything worked perfectly, and under the setting sun, I hauled everything back to the van.

Then I just sat in the van, on the shoulder of the road, ready to go, but not sure where to. South or north? The engine was idling.

The easiest thing to do was to pull out and go forward. I was facing north, toward Clearview, so I'd be heading home. I looked to the west and saw the setting sun was now turning red. A dark, deep red. Night would soon fall and that triggered a new option. I considered camping for another night. Maybe Crater would come back and answer some of my questions. Maybe those answers would help me make a decision.

But I realized that he'd already come back, last night, when I was sleeping. He'd come back and drawn the salamander in the dirt. The salamander that Fire stole from Water. The salamander that made my dad laugh.

I made a U-turn and headed south.

Chapter Eight

NIGHT FELL AND the only lights around were the beams from my headlights raking the pockmarked road in front of me. Again, I expected to see trucks, but I didn't. Over the ocean, I saw millions of stars, a panorama of gold specks which ended at the dark horizon.

As the reality of heading into the unknown settled over me, I started to think about what lay ahead. The first town I'd hit, meaning a town with people, would be Yachats. It was three hundred miles south. If I drove half the night and slept the other half, I'd arrive at dawn. But did Crater want me to go that far south? Or did he expect me to find whatever it was he wanted me to find before that?

My visa was only good for the Swan Peninsula so if I drove all the way to Yachats, the police there would arrest me. And there was also the possibility that the Fibs could pull me over anywhere along the line and that was definitely the worst-case scenario. Fibs were far more aggressive than local police. That's why they were the law of the Territory.

I KNEW A little about Yachats from my study of the Territory. Before the Virus, it'd been a tourist town. In the summer, vacationers would walk its beaches, swim its slice of the cold Pacific, and hike its coastal forests. In the winter, they'd stay in Yachats' mountain lodges, and ski and snowboard.

But now Yachats fended for itself. More so than most towns in the Territory. And because it was self-sufficient, it wasn't very active on the Line. That was why I didn't know much about the place. I did remember that it survived on fishing. Salmon, trout, and smelt. It traded some of its catch to other towns, but mostly traded within its own borders.

THE MILES PASSED and just when I thought I'd never see a truck or any other vehicle on the road, I saw red lights up ahead. Tail lights. I felt relief. I wasn't alone.

As I approached the taillights, I saw that they belonged to a tank truck, which meant the truck was hauling either water or fuel. My guess was water. The aqueduct system had ended about a hundred miles back, so water headed farther south would have to be trucked. I rolled down my window to see if I could smell gas or diesel. I didn't smell either and concluded the truck was hauling water. I passed it and watched its headlights fade in my rearview mirror as I left it behind.

A few miles later, I passed another truck. Again, a tank truck hauling water. Then I passed another and I began to wonder why I wasn't passing trucks hauling other goods. I passed three more tank trucks and my thoughts jumped to Crater. Was this what he'd wanted me to see?

I started calculating. I wanted to figure out the frequency of trucks it'd take to haul water to Yachats and to the towns south of it. Florence, Dunes City, Reedsport, Winchester Bay, Lakeside, North Bend, Charleston, Bandon, Langlois and Port Orford. Water had to be trucked to these towns because they weren't connected to Corolaqua's aqueducts. I knew how much water Corolaqua pumped out and I remembered the rough estimates I'd come up with for each town's population.

As I passed another tank truck, and then another, I started running some numbers: The amount of water each truck carried, the amount of water each town required, and the number and frequency of trucks I'd seen so far. I also took into consideration some of the other facts I remembered from my study of the Territory. Like how much water the farmers outside of North Bend used and how much water the tiny population of Langlois used for their apple orchards. I marshaled all the facts and began to calculate the frequency of tank trucks that I should *expect* to see on this road.

I passed two more tank trucks and, twenty miles later, I passed three more.

I continued to crunch the numbers, but halfway to Yachats, the long day spent repairing the pump caught up to me, so I pulled over and fell asleep.

Three hours later, I awoke to find one question dominating my thoughts. How far south did Crater want me to go? Dawn would be rising in about an hour and I'd be in Yachats in three. Had I already found what he wanted me to find? The trucks hauling water? I didn't know, and there was only one way to find out, so I pulled back on the road and continued south.

I passed twenty-four more tank trucks before hitting the outskirts of Yachats. I didn't pass any other kind of truck. I *did* pass single tank trucks headed in the *other* direction and from their speed and the way they swayed on the road, I could tell they were empty. They were headed north to reload.

Closing in on Yachats, I began to see signs of life.

Close to the road, I saw crumbling motels with clothes-lines and bicycles out front and vegetable gardens growing on the adjacent land. Then I saw old farm-houses, shacks, and ramshackle barns speckled across the countryside. Up in the rolling hills, I caught glimpses of dilapidated homes.

But something was odd. It didn't hit me immedi-ately, but took a good number of miles to make an im-pact. I should've been spotting signs of a fishing town. Boats, boat hitches, boat trailers, fishing equipment, bait farms, and fishing nets. But I didn't see any of those things. Instead, I saw truck parts strewed in fields, yards, driveways, etc. Engine blocks, exhaust pipes, truck tires, and parts that I didn't recognize be-cause I didn't know much about trucks.

Yachats was looking like a truck town. Could my study of the Territory have been that far off? Benny had confirmed that Yachats was an autonomous fish-ing town. Even though the town rarely used the Line, when it did, its communications verified that it was a fishing town.

I MADE IT into Yachats proper, and its small down-town area. Here, I saw what I expected to see. Small shops that sold food and clothes and Remnants, and a few storefront repair and trade shops. But I also saw garages with repair bays and, inside those bays, I saw truck cabs with their hoods open and mechanics at work.

I passed a few people on the streets and they glanced at my van. I hoped to make it through Yachats before they called the police. I passed a two-story building, maintained better than the other buildings, and I had no doubt that this was the Town Hall. I debated whether to pull over, head inside, and ask when Yachats had become a truck town. At the same time, I knew that I had no real evidence to prove that Yachats had ever been anything other than a truck town. I thought I knew the Territory, but maybe I didn't. I knew the 'map' of the Territory (and it was a poor map at that), but not the Territory itself.

Then I looked past the Town Hall, up into the hills, and I saw something that instantly changed everything I knew about the Territory. I was stunned. *And* I was sure that this was what Crater had wanted me to see.

Chapter Nine

I DROVE UP into the hills, toward a huge swath of cleared land. But it wasn't the cleared land that had shocked me. It was the massive storage tanks that covered that land. Five million gallon tanks, ten million gallon tanks, and twenty-five million gallon tanks. And I knew exactly what was in those tanks.

Water.

But why was it being stored here? And why didn't anyone know about it?

I didn't want to risk driving into the storage facility, which was teeming with trucks, so I headed up into the hills above it. I'd check it out from up there. I followed small winding roads up, passing a few old lodges and abandoned campgrounds. I took a few wrong turns, before I found myself on a road that ran above the storage area *and* parallel to it. It didn't have a direct view of the clearing so I decided to pull over and hike into the woods below the road.

It didn't take me long to find a good vantage point. I saw an orderly process unfolding below me. Single tank trucks pulled up to storage tanks and unloaded their water, while double and triple tank trucks pulled up and loaded up on water. Flagmen waved the trucks up and down the lanes and kept the whole process moving.

I was surprised to see double and triple tank trucks. On my way down, I hadn't seen any. So it didn't take a genius to figure out that they must all be heading south with their full loads. But why? The towns south of Yachats had plenty of water from the three desalination plants in the southern part of the Territory.

In addition to that anomaly, there was another. I was staring at way more water than Corolaqua was pumping out. The number of storage tanks meant that water was being trucked into Yachats from other desalination plants. And not just from the Willapa Bay plant up north, but also from those plants down south and that made no sense at all. Why would water be coming in from the south, then going back out *to* the south?

I wanted some answers, but I couldn't risk questioning a trucker. Truckers weren't Fibs themselves, but they might as well have been. They were licensed by the Fibs, so they acted like another set of eyes and ears for them. If a trucker suspected that I was in Yachats without a visa, he'd report it to the Fibs and I'd be jailed as a deserter. That meant five years in the penitentiary in Devinbridge.

I DROVE BACK into town. I had decided that I'd question a shopkeeper. And if that shopkeeper asked me questions of his own, I'd tell him that I'd driven down from Clearview to meet with Yachats' Councilmen about a water quality problem. My Corolaqua van would be proof that my story was true.

I parked on the main street, grabbed an empty bag from under my seat, and headed into a vegetable shop. The shopkeeper was short, thick, and grave looking. He eyed me suspiciously, which I'd expected since I was an outsider, but what I didn't expect was the hostility he radiated.

I perused the bins of vegetables. Carrots, lettuce, tomatoes, and peppers. The shopkeeper was going through a ledger, but kept glancing at me. I put some carrots in my bag and turned to him, ready to launch into small talk, but he beat me to it.

"Corolaqua?" he said. "What brings you to Yachats?" He'd already made note of my van and he wasn't waiting to get right to the point. I realized that I'd picked the wrong shopkeeper, but it was too late to back out now.

"Came down to check on the water quality," I said.

"Kind of dicey, driving through the wilderness," he said. "Why didn't you use the Line?"

"I have to take samples."

"We couldn't do that for you and truck 'em up?"

This guy wasn't going to let anything go.

"You need the right equipment," I said, and brought the carrots to the counter, ready to get out.

"You could've sent the equipment down with a trucker."

"Yeah, but you need to know how to use it or else we can't trust the samples."

He didn't respond to that and his silence told me he wasn't buying any of my story. He put the carrots on the scale, and I accepted that he was going to report me to the police as soon as I stepped out of his shop. Once that sunk in, I decided I might as well ask him a question and get something out of my foolish visit.

I was too wary to ask him directly about the water so I said, "When did Yachats go from a fishing town to a truck town?"

"Who told you we were a fishing town?"

"That's what I'd always heard," he said.

"Guess you always heard wrong."

I handed him a few coins and he gave me change then looked back down at his ledger. He didn't say another word.

I walked out without having learned anything new and now I had no choice but to leave town. My bet was the shopkeeper was already on the phone to the police. I got into my van, ready to flee, but found that I couldn't do it. Not yet, anyway. Maybe the coward label from last night was still too vivid.

I wanted some answers so I decided to go to where the answers were.

I headed up to the storage facility.

I should've headed back to Clearview.

Chapter Ten

I ENTERED THE facility and followed the wide road that ran down the center. I remembered the layout from my perch in the hills so I knew where I wanted to go. A parking area in the southwest corner. There, I'd seen truckers park their trucks and head into a nearby building. That building was probably a place for them to stretch their legs. My plan was to try talk to a trucker there.

I turned onto a smaller lane and passed trucks loading up on water and flagmen guiding trucks through intersections. Some of the flagmen glanced at me, but none stopped me. That should've been enough to make me suspicious, but I chalked it up to my Corolaqua van. I told myself that a van from a water plant fit right in when I should've told myself this was way too easy.

I made it to the parking area and saw eight trucks parked side by side. Two had drivers sitting in their cabs. I parked near the building and decided that instead of going inside like I'd originally planned, it'd be safer to talk to one of these drivers. He might be more likely to talk without other drivers around. The closest of the two was in the sixth truck down.

I got out of my van and walked past the trucks' snub-nosed hoods. I circled out a little so the driver in the sixth truck could see me approaching. I passed the alley between the third and fourth truck and thought I saw movement at the back end. I ignored it. A bad decision.

The driver in the sixth truck spotted me and he looked wary, but not hostile, so I continued forward and moved toward his cab. I hoped he'd roll down his window, but instead, he looked at his side view mirror. I glanced to the back of his truck to see what he was checking out, thinking it might just be a reflex on his part, but I'd never been more wrong. My luck had just run out. A brown uniform was moving toward me. A Fib.

I don't why I did what I did next. I could've stayed put and let the Fib question me. I could've used my job at Corolaqua to explain why I was here. I was a water man checking out a water storage facility. My story would've eventually unraveled and I would've been jailed as a deserter, but staying put and telling that story would've been better than what I decided to do.

I ran.

I BOLTED OUT from between the trucks, raced toward my van, but it was already too late for that. Another Fib was blocking my way. I veered away from him and raced toward the storage tanks, picturing the facility as I remembered it from above. I sprinted east, toward the large refueling island at the edge of the woods. I'd use the tangle of trucks at the island as cover, then disappear into the thick forest behind the facility.

I didn't look back, but I was sure the two Fibs were behind me.

A slow moving truck cut me off, so I hurled myself to the ground, rolled under its tank, caught a glimpse of the two Fibs behind me, then rolled out on the other side.

I scrambled back to my feet, raced around the storage tank in front of me, across a lane, around another tank, then alongside a moving truck. I passed a flagman, but he didn't stop me, and I wondered if the flagmen had been alerted in advance. Had the Fibs been watching me since I'd entered town? But what were they doing in Yachats in the first place?

I made it to the refueling island where half a dozen trucks were filling up. I didn't see any Fibs and I weighed whether to change my plans and double back to my van. I decided against it for fear of running right back into their hands, and I sprinted between the trucks and into the woods.

I RAN UP into the hills, crunching leaves and twigs underfoot, hoping that the Fibs weren't following those sounds. As I raced deeper into the forest, the horrible truth set in. Even if I escaped the Fibs for now, they'd eventually catch up with me. In Yachats, in the wilderness, or in Clearview. But I kept going.

After about twenty minutes, I slowed down and looked back. I didn't see anyone heading up the hill, but it was hard to know for sure because the forest was so dense. I continued forward and weighed my next move and as I did, I caught a glimpse of a lodge, about a quarter mile up the hillside. If the lodge was inhabitable, families might be living there, and if they were, one of them might have a car. That wasn't guaranteed, as cars were a luxury, but this was a truck town, so people here might know how to keep cars running. My plan was simple. Hike to that lodge, steal a car, and head back to Clearview.

I MOVED CAUTIOUSLY through the forest, toward the lodge. Each time I heard a burst of rustling leaves, I stopped, glanced around for Fibs, but it was always just a squirrel or rabbit scurrying away. I started to think less about the Fibs and more about Crater. Had I seen what he'd wanted me to see or did he want me to go even farther south?

I made it to the back of the lodge and, from the safety of the woods, I started to check it out. The dark forest was now my ally. I saw laundry lines, weighed down by wet clothes, strung across the back lawn. Kids' toys were scattered about.

Families *were* living here.

The lodge itself was a three-story wooden building that, before the Virus, would've been called rustic. Now, it was dilapidated. As I moved around it, toward the front, the parking lot came into view and my simple plan crumbled.

I *did* see a couple of cars, but I also saw five SUVs. Fib SUVs. Brown with green stripes running down the sides. The green symbolized the Territory, that narrow stretch of land along the coast. I now realized that the two Fibs who'd hunted me down were part of a larger contingent. But why were they here? Had I driven right into some sort of crisis? And that thought made me angry. At Crater. He was the one who'd led me into this.

But then I saw something that made me forget all about my anger. Victor Crow stepped out of the lodge. What the hell was *he* doing here? He was the Territory's top cop, the leader of the Fibs, and as I watched him and two other Fibs amble toward one of the SUVs, I reached one definitive conclusion. I'd stumbled into something way over my head.

Chapter Eleven

I HAD MET Victor Crow five years ago. There'd been a rumor circulating around Clearview that the marauders were going to attack the Corolaqua plant and within days of the start of that rumor, Crow and three dozen Fibs swarmed into town to protect the plant. During the day, they dominated Clearview, and that didn't stop at night. But at night, it was more personal. They stayed in people's homes. Including the Levingworths', which was where I met Crow.

RICK LEVINGWORTH WAS working on a software program and he needed help with it, so he asked to come over.

Though Benny was my only friend, Rick was family. After my father's murder, I lived with the Levingworths for many years. Even though I begged Mrs. Levingworth to let me move back home, she didn't let me go until I was seventeen. The result was that Rick was forced to share his house and his parents with me. He'd been an only child and now he suddenly had a brother. And it didn't help that Mrs. Levingworth, *his* mom, acted like she was *my* mom and treated me as if I were her son. When it came to presents, attention, and even love, she never favored him over me.

And not only did I ruin Rick's home life, but I also ruined his life at school. As soon as I moved in, kids at school started making fun of him. He was permanently linked to the weird kid. They'd taunt him and tease him and when it got to be too much, he'd fight back. Rick was strong and fearless so it was always his tormentors who'd end up with the bloody noses and fat lips. But I knew Rick's punches were really meant for me. After decking a kid, he'd sometimes scan the crowd of kids watching and he'd lock eyes with me. He didn't look triumphant. He looked angry as if he were telling me that the punches he'd just unleashed were meant for me instead of the kid on the ground. I was the one who deserved to be laid out flat, dazed and bloodied.

Still, Rick never taunted me or punched me. But he didn't defend me either. At school, he didn't speak to me and, at home, he ignored me. And that's how it stood for the first six years of our forced brotherhood. Then everything changed.

IT WAS THE last day of school, eighth grade, and I was supposed to go home with Benny. Jack Forman was having an end-of-school-year party at his house and Rick was heading over there. Benny and I weren't invited.

After school, Jack changed his mind and invited me. He wasn't one of the kids who regularly ambushed me, so I wasn't suspicious. Maybe Mrs. Levingworth had been right all along. She was always saying that one day the kids would come around. Maybe today was that day.

I didn't have the guts to ask Jack if Benny could come to the party, too. I was too happy for my own reversal of fortune. So I told Benny that I'd come over tomorrow and I ignored his disappointment. I con-

vinced myself that if I made headway with some of
these kids, he'd benefit, too.

I took off with Jack and five other kids, and one of
those kids was Gary Ledic. That should've tipped me
off. Before Ledic grew into a nasty adult, he'd been a
mean kid. A mean kid who reveled in plotting and executing cruel pranks. In elementary school, he'd told
Benny that he'd seen some electronic Remnants in
Grainer's boathouse. The boathouse had been abandoned for fifty years so Benny imagined that it might
just hold some hidden treasures. Benny went to check
it out and Ledic locked him in. For two days, everyone
in Clearview thought marauders had killed Benny. But
Ledic bragged so much about his deed that the truth
got out and Benny was rescued.

I HEADED TO Jack's house with Jack, Ledic, and four
other kids. We cut through Glenn Field Woods, but
when we were crossing the bridge over the Mory Aqueduct, the kids all stopped. I didn't know why and
thought that maybe they were going to do some kind
of end-of-school-year ritual. I realized I was completely
wrong exactly one second later when Ledic stepped up
to me and said, "Why are you always studying?"

"I'm not," I said.

"Liar," he snorted, and shoved me into the bridge's
railing.

I looked over at Jack, hoping that the invitation to
the party was still genuine, but when he grinned at me
and all the kids closed ranks around me, I accepted the
harsh reality that I'd walked right into another ambush. *And* I could tell this one was different. It wasn't
going to be just punches to the gut and face, followed

by laughter.

"We don't want you back next year," Ledic said.

"Come on, Gary," I said. "Let's just go to the party."

Right then, Bill Ely and Walt Becket lunged for my legs and Ledic grabbed my arms, and they pinned me back against the bridge's railing. I tried to free myself, but I couldn't. I could've handled any one of them, but all three were too much.

Ledic looked at the other kids and said, "So you got the story down, right? We got here and dared each other to walk on top of the railing. Then it was Roy's turn and he was doing good until he got all scared and tripped and fell."

Fear suddenly swept up from the pit of my stomach. It was a hundred foot drop to the concrete channel below and the channel was empty. There'd be no water to cushion my fall. Ledic wanted me dead and he was going to make it happen right here. I tried to think straight.

Ledic repeated, "You got the story down, right?"

The kids all nodded and I kicked out as hard as I could, freeing one of my legs and knocking Bill off balance. Ledic and Walt instantly tightened their grips on me and Bill, now angry, punched me in the balls. I grunted in pain and doubled over.

"Let's finish this up," Ledic ordered, and the three of them wrestled me onto the top of the railing and pinned me down. I had to stop struggling. Any wrong move now and I'd tumble off into the concrete below.

Ledic hovered over me, his face lit up with smug satisfaction. I'd die in the Mory Aqueduct and Ledic would be proud of his achievement. He'd relish it for years.

Ledic looked to Bill and Walt. "On three," he said.

I hoped that a rush of water would fill the aqueduct below, but I knew that no water would flow through the Mory Aqueduct that day.

"One," Ledic said.

I braced myself.

"Two."

Bill and Walt moved their arms to my side, ready to shove me over.

"Three—"

"Stop!" It was Rick's voice, and he sounded angrier than I'd ever heard him. Angrier than when he yelled at his mom for showering more affection on me than on him.

"This is none of your fucking business," Ledic said.

"Get away from him," Rick said as he stepped up to Ledic.

"Why you defending this piece of shit? We're doing you a favor."

Ledic was right. If I died, Rick would have his life back. But Rick said, "Because he's part of my family. That's why."

And that hit me in the heart. I felt it. It bonded us forever. Not because I thought Rick and I were now friends, but because of exactly what he'd said. I was part of the Levingworth family.

Rick shoved Ledic away from me, grabbed one of my legs, and pulled me off the railing.

I toppled onto the bridge, scrambled to my feet, and saw that all the kids were staring at Ledic. They wanted him to fight back.

Rick was waiting, too, glaring at Ledic, daring him to escalate this.

Ledic swung at Rick who dodged the punch and threw his own. It exploded into Ledic's nose and we all

heard the pop of cartilage as Ledic's head flew back and he crumbled to the ground.

Rick looked around to see if anyone else wanted a broken nose. None of the kids said anything. They were staring down at Ledic who was looking up at the sky, his eyes watering and glazed over, blood oozing from his nose and running down his face.

Rick turned to Jack, "Benny wants to come to your party, too. You got a problem with that?"

Jack didn't.

THE PARTY WAS okay. Rick hung out with the other kids and I hung out with Benny. Nothing changed between the other kids and me, but everything changed between Rick and me. It wasn't that we became blood brothers or anything like that, but his attitude toward me changed. He no longer resented me, he accepted me, and I wanted to pay him back for that. I wanted to show him that, yes, I was part of his family. I paid him back through computers.

KIDS RESENTED ME, but envied my knowledge of computers. I could fix them better than Jim Givens, whose job it was to fix them. I learned how to fix computers from manuals my dad had salvaged over the years and, for a while, I was obsessed with computers.

A few families in Clearview were lucky enough to have computers that worked and they used them for accounting or watching movies or playing games or listening to music. But that was about it. And when those computers broke down, these families held on to them, hoping Jim Givens could eventually fix them. But re-

placement hardware was hard to come by. Those kinds
of Remnants turned up less and less, so over the decades there were fewer and fewer working computers.

Computers were also part of Corolaqua's water pu-
rification system. They ran simple software. Simple
enough that Jim could work on it if necessary. A set of
instructions about the software had been passed down
to him from Clearview's previous computer worker
and that worker had gotten it from his predecessor.
The focal point of Jim's job was to keep Corolaqua's
computers working, so the one thing he knew well was
this set of instructions. (I'd concluded that fuel towns
and electric towns must've also had computers that
still worked, also with someone in charge of their up-
keep, but I didn't know for sure. I did know that every
town in the Territory had a computer connected to the
Line.)

Now, when it came to any other kind of software,
the story was entirely different. Jim could rarely fix the
problem, and knowledge of how to fix software was
impossible to track down. Software itself was even
more impossible to track down. That's why Jim's number one job was to make sure he never lost the knowledge needed to keep Corolaqua's primitive set-up running.

But I didn't need to track down new software. I
could fix, modify, or improve all kinds of software and
I could write new software. My obsession with computers started while I was living with the Levingworths. There, I taught myself programming and
learned how to modify the software behind computer
games. A few years later, I'd progressed to designing
new games.

So I ended up paying Rick back by teaching him

about computer games. During the summer that followed the Mory Aqueduct confrontation, I rebuilt a computer and gave it to him. Then I showed him how to play all the computer games I'd collected, modified, or designed. Within a year, his computer ran the best games in Clearview. Every kid wanted to play them.

For Rick and me, those games became our common ground and, as the years passed, computers, themselves, became our common ground. Rick developed a talent for programming and I fed that talent. After we finished high school, he became the go-to guy for software help and, if there was a problem he couldn't fix, I'd help him.

The day Victor Crow walked into Rick's house was one of those days when Rick couldn't fix a problem.

HE WAS WORKING on a project for Ellen Sanchez, the phone operator in Clearview. Before the Virus, parent switches in cities ran all phone service. The parent switches controlled the remote switches in small towns (like Clearview), but after the Virus killed off the cities, no one was left to operate the parent switches, so all phone service broke down.

Decades later, when the Territory finally stabilized, a few towns figured out how to manually operate the remote switches and a basic kind of phone service was restored. But you could only call within your own town. This was the system that Ellen Sanchez inherited from her predecessors. But unlike them, she wasn't satisfied with running the phone system like it'd always been run. She'd been one of the smartest students in school (though she'd kept that hidden), but now wanted to apply her smarts. She wanted to computerize the mechanical system of switching, so she began to work on an algorithm to do that.

It took her a while, but she came up with one. Then she asked Rick to convert it into a computer program and it took him a while, too, but he came up with one. Ellen implemented the program and it worked pretty well, but it had a few bugs. Some calls weren't going through. So she asked Rick to do more work on it and he asked me to come over and help.

RICK AND I were going through the original coding of the algorithm. We were in the basement and two Fibs were upstairs. These were two of the three dozen in town, preparing for the rumored marauder attack. Mrs. Levingworth was hosting them and so far they'd pretty much ignored Rick, which was fine with him.

I went upstairs to use the bathroom and I heard the front door open and close. Then a voice said, "Are we alone?" The voice was deep and unassailable, the voice of a man who didn't like to be questioned.

"No, sir," came the answer.

"Then clear the house," the voice said.

I headed back to the basement and told Rick that the Fibs were about to kick us out. We'd have to work at my house. So he started downloading the program but didn't get too far when the basement door opened.

I saw polished black boots descending the stairs. The boots gave way to a pair of crisp brown pants and a pressed brown shirt. The Fib uniform. Only this uniform was more distinguished than all the other uniforms I'd seen around town. It wasn't decorated with medals or signs of rank, but it still looked like it belonged to someone in command. Maybe it was the silver belt buckle that gave that impression. A polished silver block with no insignia, perfect in its simplicity and beauty.

The man behind that silver buckle made it to the bottom of the staircase. Victor Crow. A big man. Composed, controlled, and confident. But there was an undertone of menace to that confidence.

"Gentlemen, you're going to have to clear out of the house for thirty minutes or so," he said.

"No problem," Rick said, glancing at the computer to see how the download was going. "Another four minutes and we'll be out of your way."

Crow's attention went to the computer. "What are you working on?"

"Helping our phone operator," Rick said.

Crow's eyes shifted from the computer to the external hard drives, then to the cables. "How are you helping the phone operator?" he said. The subtext was clear: Don't lie to me.

Rick, nervous, glanced at me, and I answered, "We're working on a computer program to route phone calls."

"Phone switching doesn't need computers. It's mechanical," Crow said.

Right then I knew that the Territory's top cop was smart. In a time when knowledge was scarce and when workers knew only what they had to know to do their jobs, he knew more than his job required. Way more.

Crow stared at me like he was waiting for further explanation. His expression was hard and I saw that menace wanting to break out.

"She came up with an automated way to do the switching," I said.

"And why did she bring you two in on it?" he said.

The only answer was that we knew software, but I sensed that blurting that out was a big mistake. Still, I had no choice. "Because I know a little about programming," I said.

I hoped that by saying 'I' instead of 'we,' I was protecting Rick. I owed him that and much more.

"That's a rare talent," Crow said. He looked at Rick, "Do you have it, too?"

Before Rick could answer, I said, "No." I was determined to bail him out.

Crow looked back at me. "And the phone operator? Does she know how to program?"

"No," I said, "That's why she came to me with the idea." I was digging my own grave, but I was keeping Rick out of his. And Ellen.

Crow stared at me for a few seconds as if he were preparing to pass final judgment. But before he could, the other Fibs came down the stairs. They didn't say a word. They probably felt the danger hanging in the air.

"Destroy the computer and other equipment," Crow said.

The two Fibs moved to the computer and one of them pushed it off the table. It crashed down onto the concrete floor and the Fib kicked in its screen with his thick boot, then stomped on it, again and again, until the computer was nothing but broken pieces of plastic and smashed circuits.

Rick and I tried not to betray any emotion.

The other Fib knocked the external drives to the floor and stomped on them, crushing them into oblivion.

Crow said to me, "We all have jobs to do and I don't know what yours is, but I know it's not programming. That's not a job." He headed back upstairs with his men in tow. He didn't have to say anything more.

There was no actual law against working on computers, but everyone in the Territory did their jobs and nothing more. That was the key to order, and order was the key to survival. Crow saw me as a threat to that order and that's what he'd basically said.

But I wasn't enough of a threat to follow up on. At least, not yet. He didn't pursue me, or Rick, or Ellen. And after he left Clearview, I never saw him again.

Until today.

Chapter Twelve

FROM THE COVER of the woods, I watched Crow and his men climb into one of the SUVs and pull out of the lodge's parking lot. I wondered if he'd come to Yachats for the same reason he had come to Clearview. The threat of a marauder attack. Or had he come because of the water? But he must've already known about the storage facility. Even though each town didn't know much about other towns, the Fibs knew everything about each and every town. It was their job to know. That's how they kept order.

I watched Crow's SUV drive down the road and out of sight, then focused back on the parking lot. The other SUVs meant that other Fibs were still in the lodge, so stealing a car was out. It'd be safer to continue hiking toward town and check houses along the way for another car. So that's what I did.

I KEPT PARALLEL to the road, but stayed hidden in the forest. I passed a few isolated houses, but none of them boasted cars. As I moved closer to town, I started to wonder if turning myself in was a better idea. If the Fibs had bigger fish to fry, like preventing a marauder attack, maybe they'd forgive my panicked escape and overlook the fact that I didn't have a proper visa. And even if they didn't overlook it, at least I'd know my fate. Five years in the penitentiary in Devinbridge.

Still, the thought of being locked up wasn't too appealing. So I convinced myself again that there was just enough chaos in the Territory that if I were able to get back to Clearview without causing any more trouble, the Fibs might forget about me or just let me go. Like Crow had done the first time around. And this line of thinking led to another decision. I wouldn't steal a car. Stealing a car meant breaking more laws and that played against settling back into Clearview without further trouble.

My new plan was to get to the Corolaqua van. If the Fibs had left it alone, I'd drive it back to Clearview. So I changed course and headed toward the storage facility. On the way, I considered just how I'd be able to drive out of Yachats without getting stopped by Fibs.

THIRTY MINUTES LATER, as I was hiking past a dilapidated house, tucked in the woods, I heard shouting. I looked back and saw a lanky, old man, wielding a shotgun and herding a woman out of a shed. The woman had beautiful lemon blond hair which was disheveled, like she'd just woken up, and she was swinging a large backpack onto her shoulders.

I slipped behind a tree and watched.

The old man was pushing the woman forward with his shotgun and yelling at her, "Get the hell off my land," even though that's exactly what she was doing. When he finally pushed her onto the road, he added, "I'm calling the police, you goddamn marauder."

At that point, the woman could've walked away. There wasn't any reason to aggravate the old man any more than he was already aggravated. But she didn't walk away. Instead, she turned back and said, "Go ahead and call the police. You get seven years for a gun. I get one for trespassing. You lose." Her defiance animated her green eyes.

"You're a goddamn crazy one," the old man shot back. Then he lifted his shotgun, taking aim at the woman's head.

"I *am* a crazy one," she said and started down the road.

I was hooked. By her fierceness. A fierceness that was as striking as her beauty.

FROM A SAFE distance, I followed her. She stuck to the open road and I stuck to the dark forest. I kept expecting her to veer into the woods and couldn't understand why she was hiking in plain sight. If the old man did end up calling the police, she'd be walking right into their hands. Maybe, she didn't care. Maybe she wasn't a deserter or a marauder.

After five minutes or so, she suddenly stopped and looked back into the woods. "Why are you following me?" she said.

I thought I was too far back to be heard, but I should've realized from her backpack that she knew which sounds belonged to the wilderness and which didn't.

I approached her. She stood her ground. "You scared?" she said.

"I'm not so sure it's a good idea for us to chat out there in the open," I said.

The hint of a grin flashed across her lips. I'd just admitted that I *was* scared. "Where are you from?" she said.

"Clearview."

"A deserter, huh?

"Not exactly."

She tilted her head and a ray of sunlight lit up her lemon hair.

"It's a long story," I said.

"Does that story explain why you're hiding in the woods?"

"I could tell it to you and you could decide for yourself."

"Okay," she said. "Let's hear it."

Chapter Thirteen

SHE JOINED ME in the forest and, as we hiked toward the storage facility, I told her my story. The heroic version. After fixing the pump, I'd continued south to try and solve a mystery. A mystery that I'd been working on for years. I told her my theory about the extra water and that I was determined to find out what was going on with it. I didn't tell her that it was really Crater who'd lured me south and I didn't tell her about the salamander in the dirt. The salamander wrapped in the memory of my father. If I had told her the truth about my travels, she might've told me the truth about hers.

But though we both lied about what brought us to Yachats, we told each other the truth when it came to our personal lives.

LILY ARON WAS from Klamath, a coastal town in what once was the Redwood National Park. Like Yachats, Klamath had been a tourist town. It was now a lumber town that supplied lumber to the Territory.

When the Virus struck, one of the tourists in Klamath had been a biology professor from the University of California at Berkeley. After the Virus, he didn't return to Berkeley. There was nothing to return to. Everyone in Berkeley was dead. So the professor made Klamath his home and helped organize the town, one of the lucky towns spared by the Virus. Then, when things stabilized, he started to study the Virus but didn't get very far. He stopped when he heard the rumors that others researching it were dying from it. He didn't want to take the risk and he had a good reason not to. His daughter.

She grew up in Klamath, healthy and happy with no worries and no real understanding of what had happened during the previous generation. Then she had a daughter of her own. Lily, the lemon haired girl, and Lily grew up under different circumstances than her mother. Lily's grandfather took her under his wing and taught her things he hadn't been able to teach to his own daughter. He'd spent so much time helping Klamath survive, that he'd neglected to pass on his breadth of knowledge to her. And when he realized that knowledge was quickly disappearing from the Territory, he vowed that he wouldn't make that same mistake with his granddaughter. He passed on what he knew to Lily and became her tutor.

But Lily's mother wasn't too keen on the tutoring. She believed that learning more than necessary could only lead to trouble. That wasn't a surprise because that was the mindset of the Territory and she'd been brought up in that milieu. But she also worried because Lily was proving to be overly curious. As a child, Lily would hike into the redwood forest with the loggers and after the loggers started their work, she'd sneak away and explore. Each section of the forest had to be certified as Virus-free before loggers could work it, but Lily would head out anyway and afterwards her mother would punish her. She'd ground her to the house. But that made Lily want to explore even more, so it wasn't long before she wanted to explore the entire Territory. The Virus didn't scare her. She'd already wandered into the wilderness and emerged unscathed.

At twenty-two, Lily requested a visa to travel up the coast. Unfortunately, by this time, her mother had become a Councilwoman and she lobbied the rest of the Councilmen to vote against it. It wasn't that tough to convince them. Town Councils issued visas only to those who had critical reasons to travel. As long as the Virus and marauders were out there and as long as the stability of the Territory was at stake, the law was clear: No one traveled without a compelling reason.

The Town Council rejected Lily's request for a visa, but her response was to travel up the coast anyway and that was the first of a series of lawless excursions. She'd had many over the years, and that alone should've tipped me off. There *had* to be more to her desire to explore the Territory than just curiosity. She wasn't the type who was just interested in sightseeing. And I should've been clued in by the fact that her grandfather, her tutor, had been a biology professor. Lily was trained to think and to seek out answers.

AS WE GOT closer to the storage facility, I told her my plan. I wanted to continue putting the pieces of my water puzzle together, but I couldn't do that with the Fibs hunting me down. I told her I had to get back to Clearview and, on an impulse, I also offered her a ride north.

To my surprise, she accepted.

So that meant I had to explain that getting the van wasn't going to be so easy and after I filled her in on that, she surprised me again. She said she'd help me get the van out of the storage facility. Well, now came the last of bit of information she needed to know before committing. I told her Victor Crow was in town and I thought I'd see some fear in her radiant green eyes, but instead I saw curiosity. She said that in all her travels, she'd never run into him. I asked her if she feared getting caught by the Fibs and she said that she'd been detained by them a few times, but always released. She suspected that her mother, who'd been a Council-woman for over a decade, played a key role in that. A reluctant role. Her mother may have hated her travels, but she still didn't want to see her only daughter in jail.

I could've pressed Lily more about why she wanted to risk helping a fugitive, but I was far too happy to have her along as a traveling companion. I'd already fallen for her easy intelligence and fearlessness, so I accepted her explanation that riding with me was better than her usual way of traveling (which was to stow away in the rigging which some truckers added to the underside of their trucks.)

WE MADE IT to that same spot I'd found earlier, the one with the good view of the facility. We counted five Fibs on duty, then I pointed out the Corolaqua van. It was still parked where I'd left it, near the small building. The good news was that no Fibs were watching it. They were focused on various clusters of storage tanks. And that seemed to bolster my theory. The Fibs were in Yachats because of a possible marauder attack.

Lily and I studied the facility, looking at it as if it were a maze. We needed to get out of that maze. The starting point was my van and the end point was the front exit, the only exit. *And* our route had to avoid the five Fibs and the flagmen.

We came up with the best route we could, but there was one Fib we couldn't avoid. He was stationed at an intersection near the exit and we had to pass through that intersection. So Lily volunteered to distract him. The plan was for me to drive the van out while she raced into the facility, in a panic, and told him that she'd just seen a couple of marauders. He'd either leave his post to check her story out, or he'd leave his post to detain her. Either way, the intersection would be temporarily clear. And if he detained her, she was sure she'd be freed like she'd always been.

We set up a rendezvous spot, then hiked down and parted ways.

I STEPPED OUT of the woods onto the facility grounds, right behind the small building. I made my way along its back wall, using it as cover, and as soon as I cleared the building, I hurried toward my van. My timing had to match Lily's, so I couldn't wait for the coast to be clear and, sure enough, a trucker stepped out of the building.

I slowed down, so I wouldn't look suspicious and he glanced at me. I kept my expression neutral, climbed into the van, started it up, and pulled out. I checked my rearview mirror and saw that the trucker was now watching my van. There was nothing I could do about that.

I snaked through the facility along the route we'd mapped out and it was all going smoothly until I found myself stuck behind a truck. A flagman was directing the truck, helping it maneuver up to a storage tank. I waited, knowing that I couldn't take another route and hoping my luck hadn't turned. We'd known that there was the possibility of a flagman being drawn from his post to help a trucker maneuver. We'd seen that from above, but it didn't happen a lot. Well, it was happening now, and then it got worse.

The flagman spotted me and started walking toward me. I saw a slim opening in front of me, so I weighed whether to floor it or not, but quickly decided against it. This wasn't a Fib. It was a flagman. So I rolled down my window.

"Fibs are looking for you, bud," he said. "Why don't you pull over?"

"What do they want with me?" I asked.

He smirked. "Like they're gonna tell me."

That comment told me everything I needed to know. Like everyone in the Territory, he wasn't fond of the Fibs, so I said, "They probably were looking for an excuse to search my van and take my Curado."

The flagman smiled and that closed the deal.

"Tell you what," I said. "You take it. Better you than them." And without waiting for an answer, I leaned over, quickly pawed through my food supplies, pulled out the bottle of Curado and handed it to him.

He checked it out, grinning and appreciating his good luck. "I've never tried it," he said.

Of course not, I thought. It'd probably cost him two years pay. "Enjoy," I said, and pulled away, right through that slim opening.

I checked the rearview mirror to see what he'd do next. He was walking back toward the front of the truck, taking his time and keeping the bottle low to his side, hidden. I was sure he was trying to figure out where to stash his prize. Somewhere out of sight of any Fib. He'd never dreamt he'd come across a bottle of the fabled liquor and he wasn't going to lose it now.

I SWUNG AROUND two more storage tanks and found myself behind a slow-moving truck. It was slow because it was a triple tank truck. I pulled to its left, checked for approaching trucks, and didn't see any. So I started to pass it and as I did, I noticed rigging underneath the tanks. The rigging was crammed with sacks. (Lily had told me the truckers added this rigging to haul extra goods that they'd sell on the side.) The whole set-up looked rough and uncomfortable. No wonder she didn't like traveling that way.

I passed the tank truck and I knew that the next left would be the moment of truth. It led to the intersection with the Fib. Hopefully, Lily had cleared him out. In terms of the timing, I was on schedule, so I felt fairly confident that my bad luck was behind me. Especially because I'd managed to talk my way out of getting pulled over.

I took the left and looked down the lane. No Fib. Great. I couldn't help speeding up a little to make sure I'd get through the intersection before he returned. I made it through and didn't see any sign of the Fib. Lily had done her job. I continued toward the exit, glancing up and down the remaining lanes, which were clear of Fibs. Still, I began to feel a little uneasy, like something was wrong. But I shrugged it off and thought about meeting Lily at the rendezvous spot, an empty campground, tucked in the hills, about a mile away.

I turned and started down the lane that would take me to the main road and I spotted Lily. This wasn't good. About a hundred yards in front of me, two Fibs had her backed up against the side of a double tank truck that was loading up on water. Lily's backpack was on the ground and it looked like the Fibs were interrogating her. They saw my van and one of them moved to the middle of the lane, drew his gun, and motioned for me to stop. But I couldn't just stop, and give myself up. I had to help Lily. It was my fault that the Fibs had captured her and I was almost a hundred percent sure that, this time, they weren't going to let her go.

Lily was up against the truck's first tank, and the second tank was hooked up to a ten million gallon storage tank. A pipe, made of industrial plastic, probably Teflon fluorocarbon (like some of the pipes at Corolaqua), connected the two. Teflon fluorocarbon was a tough plastic able to withstand the powerful pressure of water gushing through it.

That pressure was going to be my weapon.

I sped up, hoping that Lily would know what to do.

The Fib saw me bearing down on him so instead of shooting at me, he raced out of the way to save himself, and at the last second, I swerved my van toward the truck, aiming for the second tank. I smashed into it and the air bag exploded from my steering wheel so I didn't actually get to see the pipe break lose but I heard the deluge and I knew that this collision had sent hundreds of gallons of water spewing.

I scrambled out of the van and ran toward the back of the storage tank. Water was flooding the entire area, and I spotted Lily running through the spray. We both sprinted past the storage tank, leaving the deluge behind.

"We have to get to the woods," I said, running across a lane.

"They're expecting that," she said.

She was right. We ran between two storage tanks and I glanced back. A Fib was crossing the lane, bearing down on us.

"I've got a better idea," she said.

"I'm all ears."

"We need to find a truck heading out. With rigging."

I remembered the triple tank truck I'd passed minutes ago. It was probably still on its way out. "I know just the truck."

We wove between the massive storage tanks, heading in that direction, until we spotted it.

"When it passes, we run for the rigging," Lily said.

The truck rolled closer.

"What if the driver sees us?" I asked.

"They have a blind spot. Toward the front of the first tank," she said. "Run straight to the front of the tank. Don't run alongside it, and he won't see us."

We sprinted to the blind spot, ducked under the tank, and crawled into the rigging beneath. We were lying next to burlap sacks packed with onions. The sacks hid us from view on the far side, but we were exposed on the near side, so we pulled some of the sacks around.

The truck rolled forward and when I saw water flowing on the lane beneath us, I knew we were passing the scene of the crash and close to exiting the facility.

Two minutes later, the truck picked up speed. We were out.

Chapter Fourteen

THE SOUND OF the truck's engine was thunderous, so we couldn't talk. After a couple of miles, the truck slowed and I said, "I turned you into a fugitive."

"I volunteered," Lily said.

I smiled. In the midst of our near disastrous escape, she still had a sense of humor. "I won't be able to give you that ride to Clearview," I said.

"I kind of figured that."

"If we stay on this truck, we're going south," I said, almost as an afterthought, maybe to assure myself that we were still in control somehow.

"How do you know?"

"It's a triple tank and I didn't see any triples or doubles when I came in from the north."

"Then they're headed east," she said.

"That's impossible."

"Well, I came up from the south and I didn't see any triple and double tank trucks either," she said. "And we know they're not going west into the ocean. That leaves east, right?"

I didn't respond. Why would trucks go east? The Territory's eastern border was thirty miles inland from the coast and past that border were two thousand miles of dead land. I went back to the thought I'd had many years ago – that the extra water was being shipped to small towns that had survived on the east coast. But just as I had concluded back then, hauling water across two thousand miles of dead land didn't make any sense. Lily had to be wrong. The water *had* to be heading south.

A minute later, the truck started rolling over a patch of rough road and we were suddenly bounced around in the rigging. It was painful. "Do like this," Lily said, putting her hands up against the bottom of the tank and pressing her back against the rigging. "Hold yourself in place, not too rigid, like your arms are shock absorbers."

I put my hands on the bottom of the tank and secured myself against the rigging. The tank felt cool from the water inside. We bumped along for a couple hundred yards until the road turned smooth again.

As the trucker neared the center of Yachats, he slowed down and stopped a number of times as he maneuvered through the various intersections. During this stretch, we could've climbed out, but we didn't. And neither of us brought up the next move. Instead, we rearranged some of the sacks so pedestrians couldn't see us and I complained about the smell of diesel. Lily said she had learned to ignore it.

The trucker ground to another stop when he hit the town's major north-south artery. We were about to get the first clue to the water's ultimate destination.

THE TRUCKER TURNED south. But this didn't mean that he'd definitely continue south, and I wondered if Lily knew that. It didn't take long for me to find out.

"If he's going east, he's going to take the 126," she said.

That meant she knew the Territory well. The 126 led inland to the 5, a highway that connected Portland, Salem, and Eugene. The 5 was a dead highway leading to dead cities. As a teen, I'd dug up an old and barely legible map of the Western states. There were no detailed maps of the Territory and I'd thought I'd discovered a rare treasure. A useful treasure. Back then, Benny and I still dreamt of exploring the Territory so I memorized this map. But unlike Lily, we never found the courage to pursue our dream.

"You want to follow the water?" she said.

"By staying under the truck?" I asked.

"That'd be the plan. For now."

I didn't answer.

WE WERE CLOSING in on the 126 and I still doubted the trucker would turn east. But regardless of whether he was headed east or south, he was headed into the wilderness. "What about food?" I asked.

"We steal a little of the trucker's food when he's sleeping," Lily said. "He'll think it's a marauder."

"Sounds like you know the drill."

"Yeah. And sometimes it even works."

"And what happens when it doesn't?"

"You go hungry."

The trucker slowed down, then started to execute a wide turn.

No doubt about it.

"East," Lily said.

Chapter Fifteen

THE NEXT STRETCH on the 126 would give us time to reconsider our decision. Not that I'd officially made a decision. I still hadn't really answered Lily, and I knew that there'd be opportunities up ahead to scramble out from under the truck. The trucker would be navigating the inland hills of the 126, and he'd have to slow down a bunch of times. Each time would be a chance to climb out and cut this trip short. But when the trucker hit the long flat stretch east of the border, we'd be stuck. Of course, that assumed that long flat stretch still existed. I'd never heard of anyone venturing past the border and coming back.

THE TRUCKER NAVIGATED the hills and neither Lily nor I said anything. The unwieldy water tanks weaved back and forth and, on the sharper curves, the trucker came to an almost complete stop.

"What do you want to do?" Lily asked.

I knew what she wanted to do. She didn't have to tell me. Lily, the fierce, would always go forward even if that meant going into uncharted territory. But I wanted more information first. Information that would ease my fear about going into uncharted territory. Information that I wasn't going to get. And she must've known what was going through my mind because, before I could answer her, she said, "If we don't like what we see out there, we can always hitch a ride back on an incoming truck."

She was right. I'd caught glimpses of trucks heading in the other direction, but I hadn't thought of them as a way back. I'd been too uneasy about the road ahead to plan ahead.

"Okay," I said. "Let's stay put." I didn't say this with any conviction. I was full of doubts. But I was willing to stick to it for now.

AS WE MOVED closer to the border, the flat stretches became longer. I wasn't sure if I wanted to go beyond the border, but I didn't say anything. Instead, I thought about the two thousand miles of dead land ahead. Inland, the Virus hadn't shown any mercy. It had killed everyone in Eugene, Boise, Phoenix, Kansas City, Denver, Santa Fe, Austin, Des Moines, Minneapolis, Chicago, Madison, and every city in between.

But the more I thought about it, the more I wondered if this could be a lie, too. Like the lie that Yachats was a fishing town. Could there be towns inland? The extra water sure pointed to it.

After twenty minutes or so, the trucker picked up speed and I knew we'd passed the border. From here, the road quickly became monotonous and Lily and I didn't talk. At this speed, the din of the engine, the whip of the wheels, the rushing wind, they all added up to a dulling numbness.

Lily stared blankly at the countryside. I didn't know if she was hypnotized by the scenery or lost in her own thoughts, but she looked to be a thousand miles away. I wasn't. I was stuck right here and was now worrying about the Virus. In the Territory, truckers used roads that they knew were free of the Virus and stuck to those roads until the Virus reared its ugly head. I was trying to convince myself that our trucker was doing just that even though he was outside the Territory.

After about ninety minutes, most of which I spent thinking that I was pushing my luck with this whole excursion, the scenery changed. We were on a six-lane freeway and the wilderness was gone. I also spotted other trucks on the freeway. Then, in the distance, when the angle was right, I caught glimpses of tall buildings, city buildings, and I realized we were approaching Eugene. I was seeing a city for the first time. I'd seen them in photos and DVDs, but never in person.

I began to wonder if Eugene was the destination for all the extra water. Were people still alive there?

The answer came quickly. Our truck skirted Eugene, and minutes later, we were back on the open road.

THE MILES PASSED and I hoped our trucker would pull over. I needed a break, to stretch my legs, to eat, to go to the bathroom. I wondered if Lily needed a break as badly as I did. Her eyes were closed, but it didn't look like she was sleeping. It looked like she'd transported herself even farther away than before, and definitely far away from doubt.

She looked serene.

I didn't have the discipline to turn off my surroundings.

MORE MILES PASSED and I could tell from the shadows on the road that we were heading southeast. We were no longer on the 5, and the truck was now using two-lane rural highways.

My back was sore from the metal rigging and the diesel fumes were short-circuiting my senses. I was more than ready for the trucker to pull over. I looked over at Lily and her eyes were still closed. She was somehow able to ignore her discomfort and keep her fierceness in check, now that it was unnecessary.

Then she suddenly opened her eyes, found mine, and smiled. That was all I needed to keep going.

THE SUN WAS setting, the air was cold, and the shadows on the road were long. My body felt numb.

The truck finally started to slow down and I saw Lily go on full alert. From my limited vantage point, I could see that we were still in the middle of nowhere, so I figured the trucker was slowing down to execute a turn or to pull over. I hoped he was pulling over, but I was quickly disappointed. He was segueing onto a small transition road which probably led to another rural highway.

But suddenly, out of nowhere, he was passing other trucks. *Parked* trucks. The transition road had led into a parking lot. Was this where the trucker was going to unload the water? He pulled into a slot between two parked trucks and cut the engine. I immediately noticed the loud ringing in my ears. The sound of the road was seared into my head.

Lily's voice cut through the ringing. "What a fun way to ride, huh?"

"You looked like you could've gone for another thousand miles."

"It's just practice. The first time I did this, I felt like

you do now. Like my brain and body had been pummeled by a concrete block."

"Let's get the hell out of this thing."

"Let's wait for the driver to get out first."

I couldn't argue with that. We'd made it this far without getting caught, no reason to get impatient now.

"I'd say we've gone about three hundred fifty miles southeast," she said. "Any idea what towns might be out here?"

She was asking out of politeness. She'd kept track of the mileage and the direction, so my bet was that she knew exactly where we were, somewhere in what used to be southern Oregon or northern California or northwest Nevada. This area was once federal land and there were *never* any towns here. This was where the Winema National Forest, the Fremont National Forest, and the Modoc National Forest all met.

"There aren't *any* towns out here," I said.

"So you think it's some kind of rest stop?"

"Never heard of rest stops in the Territory so it's hard to believe there'd be any out here. What about a new town, one that came together after the Virus?"

Just then, we heard the driver's door open, and that ended our conversation. A few seconds later, we heard the door shut, and we waited until the driver's footsteps faded away. Then Lily said, "Let's get some answers."

Chapter Sixteen

WE CLIMBED OUT of the rigging and checked up and down the aisle between our truck and the one next to it. There was another row of parked trucks in front of us and behind us was the forest. More importantly, we were alone, so before anyone could spot us, we headed into the forest. I was stiff and sore and the ringing in my ears wouldn't let up. I also couldn't escape the odor of diesel, but in the forest, I detected another odor, faint, hovering under the diesel. I couldn't tell what it was.

When we were about thirty yards into the woods, we turned back and surveyed the parking lot. Our view was blocked by the trucks. There were dozens of them. All double and triple tank trucks. Why were they here?

WE CIRCLED THROUGH the woods, following the border of the parking lot. The rows of trucks gave way to a large, low-slung building. Steam was pouring out of exhaust fans on its roof, and I finally recognized the odor lingering under the diesel fumes. Fried food.

We moved closer to the building and through its windows, we saw truckers eating. This was a diner. The Territory didn't have diners. Of course, this wasn't the Territory, but this *was* the middle of nowhere. Then I realized that this wasn't just a diner. It was part of the infrastructure for the transportation of that extra water.

Just as Yachats was.

"So it *is* a rest stop," Lily said.

"On the way to where?" I said.

"Let's ask one of the workers," she said, as she watched a waitress bringing food to a table. "Where do you think they live?"

I moved back a couple of yards and motioned for her to take a look. She stepped back and saw what I'd seen a few minutes ago when we were approaching the diner – a series of rundown trailers which ran along the edge of the woods.

WE STATIONED OURSELVES so that we had a direct view of the diner's back entrance. Our plan was to approach one of the diner's workers and ask him or her about the rest stop and the water. How we'd know who'd be willing to talk to us wasn't clear, but we set up shop and waited.

A couple workers stepped outside and started talking to each other in short bursts, like they were bored and didn't want to put in the effort to talk. They looked to be in their fifties, set in their ways, and neither of them looked friendly. After ten minutes or so, they headed back inside.

Twenty minutes later, a woman in her forties, looking exhausted, stepped outside and dragged herself over to one of the trailers. She didn't look too friendly either.

Then five minutes later, we saw a woman in her early twenties step outside and slam the door behind her. She whipped off her ponytail holder and vigorously shook out her long brown hair. She looked angry and ready to pick a fight. Right behind her, an older man stepped out. He was large and lumbering and walked with a stoop, as if life had beat him down. He began to talk to the woman. He might've been her husband but the age difference and the dynamic between them told me that he was her father. And it looked like he was telling her that everything would be okay. She listened to him and softened, her slender body relaxing, but as soon as he went back inside, she looked angry again, like she knew everything would never be okay. Ever.

Lily and I both thought that this woman might be angry enough to tell us where all the trucks were headed.

THE WOMAN MARCHED toward one of the trailers and we stepped out of the forest. We were ready with an explanation about why we were here. We'd come up with it while we were scoping out the workers. But when I saw this woman up close, I knew that launching into our explanation wasn't the right move. With her, it'd be better to get to the point. So I blurted out, "Can you help us?"

"You're not truckers," she said. "Are you marauders?" She was wary, but curious.

"No," Lily said.

"Who are you?"

"No one special," I said. "We're trying to make it through the dead land to see if there are towns on the other coast."

"How'd you get this far?" she fired back.

"We hitched," Lily said.

"No trucker'd give you a ride."

"One did," I said.

"I don't believe you. He'd lose his job and they got it easy."

Now, it was time to lay out our explanation. "We bribed him," I said. "We found some medicine in an old hospital – medicine that his wife needed and we traded it for a ride." This slowed her down. She was weighing it. Everyone knew that medicine was rare.

"What happens if you're caught on the road without a visa?" she asked.

"We haven't been caught," Lily said.

But I could tell that she didn't really want to know what would happen to *us*. She wanted to know what would happen to *her*. What would happen if *she* ran away and was caught without a visa? So I answered *that* question. "You get five years in jail," I said. "Then you go back to where you came from."

She relaxed a little, then smirked and said, "So the trucker said he'd take you to the other coast, huh?"

"He didn't say exactly how far he'd take us. But he took the medicine and gave us a ride," I said.

"Well, you traded that medicine for a dead end," she said, her brown eyes sparkling. The joke was on us. "The trucks go to Black Rock, about another hundred fifty miles away, then back to the Territory. Black Rock is as far east as you're gonna get."

Lily and I looked at each other, confused. Black Rock was a dry lakebed in the middle of a desert. It was the largest flat mud surface on Earth. There was literally nothing there. Why would trucks be hauling water to Black Rock?

Chapter Seventeen

SARAH INVITED US into her trailer. The way she put it was that if we continued to talk out here, we'd have to deal with some of her coworkers and they "hated strangers more than each other."

Once inside, it became clear that she wanted advice. She dreamt of running away and she wanted to know how to avoid the Fibs. She told us that a few truckers had offered to whisk her away, but their offers came with strings attached. They wanted her to stay with them and, for her, that meant going from the prison of the diner to the prison of their houses. And if she ran away from them, they'd report her to the Fibs and she'd have to start her new life in the Territory as a fugitive.

So she'd come up with another plan. From the time she was a child, she'd known the forest was safe from the Virus. All through her childhood and teen years, she and her friends had dared each other to go deeper and deeper into the woods and not one of them had ever contracted the Virus. So over the years, she'd trained herself to survive in the wilderness, preparing for the day that she'd hike away from the rest stop on her own, without help from any truckers. She had learned how to trap small animals and cook them on open flames. She'd experimented with wild plants and knew which were edible and which made her sick. And she'd also learned to dress wounds in case she injured herself. But even with all this preparation, she'd never left.

And I understood why. Fear was more powerful than dreams.

Sarah offered us food and, as we ate, she answered our questions about the rest stop. The seven families who worked here, including her and her dad, owned it. Food for the diner was trucked in once a week, but all the other trucks that stopped here were water trucks.

I asked her why the rest stop was even here if the water was only going as far as Black Rock. The distance from Yachats to Black Rock was five hundred miles. Truckers could do the round trip in one or two days. They didn't need a rest stop. They made way longer trips in the Territory.

She explained that the truckers weren't allowed to deliver water to Black Rock at night. So when they weren't going to make it before nightfall, they'd stop at the rest stop, have a meal, spend the night in their trucks, then drive the hundred fifty miles left in the morning.

We asked a few more questions before I asked the only question that mattered. Who were the truckers delivering the water to?

Sarah said she had no idea, but I guess she could tell that we badly wanted an answer, so she told us her father's theory. He believed that, at night, trucks drove into Black Rock from the east and hauled the water inland. He thought that there *were* towns inland but that they'd sprung up way after the Virus so they weren't like the towns in the Territory. They were wilder and unorganized and didn't have the resources to purify their own drinking water.

"What do the truckers say?" I asked.

"They never talk about the water," she said.

"What about Black Rock? Do the truckers say there's a water storage facility there?" For her father's theory to be true, the water had to be stored there so that trucks could come in from the east and haul it away.

"Like I said, they never talk about the water and we all learn not to ask about it." Then she suddenly asked us about the marauders, like she somehow connected them to water, and I noticed that her eyes lit up when she mentioned them. Lily told her the standard stuff and I could see that this was a letdown for Sarah, so I added, "I met a marauder." That got her attention. It also got Lily's attention because I still hadn't told *her* about Crater.

"He wanted to know about the water, right?" Sarah asked me.

She *did* connect the marauders to water. Why?

"You're not really headed east to see if towns are there," she said. "You're following the water."

"That's right," I said.

She looked toward the diner, like she was weighing whether to open up, then she looked back at us, ready to tell us the secret that she'd been dying to tell us all along.

"THREE YEARS AGO, when I was in the forest, training myself for the getaway, the one I still haven't managed to make," she said, "I trapped a rabbit. I was skinning it and gutting it and thought someone was watching me. Maybe Brian, who had a crush on me. I called out and no one answered. So I built my fire and cooked the rabbit.

"When I started to eat, he came out. Except it wasn't

Brian. It was a marauder. And he told me he was impressed with what he'd seen. He asked me if I wanted to join the marauders. I wanted to escape, but I didn't want to be a marauder. I told him that I was learning how to survive in the wilderness, so I could make it *through* the wilderness and into the Territory. I wanted to live in a town, not the wilderness.

"He accepted that and then told me he was here to find out about the water. So I told him about Black Rock. Why not? He didn't seem like a bad person, like those stories you hear about the marauders. He hadn't attacked the rest stop or the trucks or stolen anything. He just wanted to find out where the water was going. Like you."

Sarah looked back to the diner, anxious. She clearly wanted to get through her story before her dad showed up. "So he said that he was going out to Black Rock to find out what was going on. He also said that he'd come back and take me to the Territory if I wanted to go. I could decide when he got back.

"He left and I began to think about it. He seemed like a good guy. But what if he was lying? What if I went with him and he wanted me to stay with him? Like the truckers. I'd have to run and then I'd be running from the marauders and that wouldn't be so good."

Sarah stopped and took a breath, "Turns out I didn't have to worry about it. He never came back."

She was upset. She had wanted to escape and she'd thought that this marauder might have been her passage out. She told us that no one had ever approached her again. When she went out into the forest, she was always on the lookout for marauders, but she was always disappointed.

SARAH CLEARED THE table and washed the dishes. Her dad's shift was almost over and she wanted us to hide in her bedroom for the night. We said we'd sleep outside, but she insisted we stay inside. She said her dad respected her privacy and would never go into her bedroom.

We settled in on blankets on her bedroom floor and, when her dad came home, I overheard their conversation and understood why Sarah hadn't run away. It wasn't because of fear. She and her dad talked about the supply of food at the diner, the number of truckers who'd come through that day, a feud with another family over work schedules, and other mundane topics, but shining through the small talk was Sarah's bond with her dad. That bond was stronger than her dream of escape.

As I let the warmth of their conversation wash over me, I noticed a DVD movie on Sarah's dresser. She had told us that their community had acquired two hundred and seventy-two movies over the years and that she had watched them over and over again. This one was "Planet of the Apes" and that movie was the story of my life.

ROUGHLY FIVE THOUSAND movies floated around Clearview. Ellen Sanchez, the phone service operator, had the biggest collection in town, one hundred or so, and it was at her house, at a birthday party, that I first saw "Planet of the Apes." I was in elementary school and it was right after my dad's murder. She'd invited me to her party because she felt sorry for me.

I watched the movie and decided it was about my father. He was like the smart astronaut in the movie,

Taylor. Taylor crash lands in the wilderness of another planet and starts to hike away from the crash site, looking for signs of life. Then apes suddenly attack him. Vicious, stupid apes. And just like Taylor, my father had ventured out into the wilderness and marauders had attacked him. Vicious, stupid marauders.

A week after the birthday party, I asked Rick if he would borrow the DVD for me. I didn't want to borrow it directly from Ellen because I didn't want other kids to taunt her for lending one of her precious DVDs to the weird kid. Rick must've borrowed that DVD for me over a dozen times. The last time, I figured out how to copy it and I didn't have to borrow it again.

As the years passed, Taylor, the astronaut, went from representing my father to representing me, and the apes went from representing the marauders to representing other kids. I was Taylor, trying to hide the knowledge I'd learned, and the kids were the apes, hunting me down and kicking the crap out of me because I knew too much.

Then, as I got older, I wasn't Taylor anymore, I was Dr. Zira, the scientist. She was the one who'd started to understand why things worked the way they did and she wanted to tell the other apes. But the apes wouldn't listen to her and, if she talked too much, they'd kill her.

Of course, I never thought that anyone in Clearview would really want to kill me. I'd decided that what had happened at the Mory Aqueduct was just kids getting out of hand. But after I started my job at Corolaqua, I discovered that I was wrong. Someone *did* want to kill me.

Chapter Eighteen

DURING MY FIRST months at Corolaqua, I tried to keep a low profile. But Frank had heard that I was good at analyzing and fixing things (that was why the Town Council had wanted me to work at Corolaqua), so he asked me to check out some of the plant's equipment. The equipment worked, but sometimes had minor hiccups which no one had been able to fix.

I studied the problems and came up with repairs. So it didn't take long for the other plant workers to resent me and their resentment quickly grew. I found out just how much during the annual Corolaqua celebration.

EVERY YEAR, COROLAQUA threw a party at Welketch Beach and invited everyone in town. It started in the evening, under the orange red sun, and went long into the night. It'd been a town ritual for forty years. People swam, played football, and soccer, and they barbecued and drank.

For every stage of my life, I had a memory associated with that celebration. When I was five, I built the biggest sandcastle in the world with my dad. When I was seven, I ended up lost and terrified in the craggy rocks of Juniper Cove and found my way back by following the voices of teens hiding from their parents.

When I was ten, I argued with Mrs. Levingworth because I wanted to stay at the party after the younger kids had already gone home. I won the argument and thought I was a grown up.

When I was fifteen, I drank alcohol for the first time and vomited. I lied to Mrs. Levingworth and told her that I'd eaten too much barbecue. And when I was seventeen, I saw Ellen making out with Brad Stall and realized that I should've made my own move that year, that Ellen was ready for a boyfriend, and now her boyfriend wouldn't be me.

But all those memories were overshadowed by one memory.

DURING THE ANNUAL celebration, Corolaqua workers all had jobs to do, from barbecuing and serving food to organizing and supervising games.

I was a lifeguard and there was nothing unusual about that. The younger workers were usually the lifeguards because they were in the best shape. And when night fell and there wasn't any swimming, only one lifeguard watched the ocean, in case teens dared each other to swim in the dark.

That night, I was the one lifeguard and I stationed myself far from the barn fire so I could see past the light of the flames. It was hard to see anything at all because the moon was a tiny sliver. I watched the sea and I listened to the waves striking the beach. I heard parents and grandparents laughing around the barn fire and, in the other direction, I could barely discern groups of teens in the darkness.

Then, between the crashes of waves, I heard a cry. A sharp cry. I looked up and down the beach, trying to pinpoint where it had come from and I heard it again. It wasn't a burst of laughter. It was a scream. And it wasn't coming from the people gathered around the barn fire. I looked out into the ocean, past the roaring waves and into the blackness, and heard another scream. I scanned the water and thought I saw movement. It was black on black, but a black separate from the ocean. Then I heard someone shout, "Help!"

I rushed forward and kept my eyes on the spot where I'd seen that movement. I sprinted into the surf, dove into the sea, and swam under the breaking waves. When I popped back up, I checked that spot again, but didn't see anything. Then I heard the cry again. It was definitely coming from out there, in the darkness. I was sure some teen had swum out and panicked.

I swam as hard as I could, barreling through the crashing waves until I made it to the calmer waters on the other side. I looked toward the spot again and I saw the teen. He went under.

I picked up my pace and checked again. The teen popped up through the water, but was quickly pulled back down. Was I watching a shark attack? Years ago, there'd been reports of shark attacks down south, but never in Clearview. I swam toward the teen, but when I looked up again, I didn't see him. I wanted him to pop up so I could confirm I was still headed in the right direction and, just as I put my head back down for the final sprint, he did. Then he was pulled under again.

I was on course, but something was weird. This time I'd noticed that the teen had his head covered. At least, that's what it looked like. But it was hard to tell in the dark. That should've stopped me and I wish it had.

I closed in on the spot, but I didn't see the teen. I dove down under the water and looked around. It was too dark to see anything.

I resurfaced and glanced around me. Nothing.

Then, a few yards in front of me, the teen popped up, and went under. His head *was* covered in something. He must've been the butt of some cruel joke. I lunged forward and the teen suddenly shot out of the water right in front of me and I grabbed him. He grabbed me back and tried to pull me under. He was panicking. He pulled hard and he was strong, and big, and I realized that he wasn't a teen.

I went down with him, then struggled to get back to the surface, trying to pull him up with me.

We both made it to the surface and I yelled for him to calm down. He was safe now. But he was already pulling me under again and, just as I began to wonder if he was doing it on purpose, someone *else* grabbed my legs. I tried to kick free, but I felt something clamp down on one of my ankles. Then the man with the covered head let me go and swam away, but I realized I was in trouble so I lunged at him, grabbed his leg, and held tight. At the same time, I tried to shake my ankle free from whatever was clamped around it.

I wouldn't let go of the man, so he pulled me along as he swam away, until I came to an abrupt and jarring stop, held back by whatever was connected to my ankle. The man kicked hard to free himself from my grip, but I viciously twisted his leg to stop him from shaking me off. For a second, he stopped struggling. I'd hurt him.

Then the clamp around my ankle started reeling me down, under the water, and the man easily kicked free of my grip. He was home free and I was buried in the ocean. The reeling stopped after a few seconds and I tried to swim to the surface, but I couldn't reach it.

The trap had been perfectly set. I was anchored in

place, under the dark sea, with no way to call for help. I could hold my breath for two, three minutes tops, so I had to do something fast. I reached down and checked my ankle. Around it, I felt a metal ring, a cuff of some kind. I felt further down and found the cuff was attached to a thick chain. I wasn't going to be able to break the cuff or the chain.

I thought about those apocryphal stories where a bear gnaws off his limb to escape a trap, but even if I could figure out a way to sever my ankle, I didn't have the time to do it. The only hope was to get to the other end of the chain and find what was anchoring it down.

I swam down, using the chain as my guide. I wanted to breath, to suck in some fresh air, but I knew I couldn't. My ears started to feel the water pressure and I began to doubt my strategy.

But it was too late to change it.

As I approached the ocean floor, about thirty feet from the surface, I felt faint. I was desperate for air and the pressure in my ears was brutal. I forced myself down to the very end of the chain and, there, I found an anchor. I couldn't see it, but I felt it. My hands moved across it, and I fought my delirium and concentrated on the facts. A mushroom anchor. Between thirty and sixty pounds. I reached around the anchor with both hands and tried to lift it. It moved, but barely.

I was going to die.

I dug my hands under the anchor, pulled myself close to it, then jerked it up. It moved and I started kicking, holding the anchor close. I breathed out. I couldn't help it. I was going to pass out. I kicked harder, clutching the anchor, hoping to get to the surface, and I breathed in water. I desperately needed air.

The anchor wanted to sink back down and take me with it, but I wouldn't let it. If I could carry the anchor to the surface, I'd live.

I kicked harder, moving up, closer to the surface, refusing to let the anchor bury me at sea.

I popped through the surface and sucked in air. I kicked and held onto the anchor, and tried to catch my breath. I wanted to yell for help, but I couldn't. Breathing took too much effort.

After about another minute or so, I started kicking toward the shore. When the water was shallow enough, I dropped the anchor and yelled for help.

FRANK HEARD MY shouts, swam out, and helped me back to shore. Later that night, Uslov Sidorov, the welder in Clearview, cut the cuff off my ankle.

I spent the rest of the weekend keeping my anger in check. I tried not to think about suspects because that made me too angry, but, as usual, I couldn't completely stop myself. I didn't have any clues to go on. Anyone in town could've acquired the anchor. Before the Virus, there were plenty of boats lining these coastal waters and that meant there were plenty of abandoned anchors. As for the cuff, it could've been salvaged from any of the thousands of abandoned police stations all over the Territory.

I did talk to Clearview's policemen, but it was clear that they weren't going to do a thing. Trevor Hunter and Elijah Toric, two of our three policemen, questioned me and treated the entire thing like it was a prank. Corolaqua workers were just having a little fun, like an old-fashioned hazing. I told them that the plant workers had never hazed anyone before and they said,

"There's always a first time." Hunter and Toric's job was to keep the peace and this didn't threaten the peace. It was just a prank, not attempted murder. They thought I couldn't take a joke and that I was a coward for making this into a big deal. So I didn't push it with them.

ON MONDAY, I went back to work. Most of the plant workers knew what had happened and most of them had the same attitude that Hunter and Toric had had. It'd been an elaborate prank. But I was hyper-aware of everyone's body language, on the plant floor, in the hallways, and in the lunchroom. I was looking for suspects. And the end of my shift couldn't come fast enough because by the end of the day everyone was starting to look like a suspect.

I headed out to the parking lot, telling myself that I had to put this behind me. As I climbed into my car, I saw Ledic's car pull in. He was working the next shift. I keyed the ignition and in my rearview mirror, I saw him getting out his car. He was always a sight to see. When Rick had defended me at the Mory Aqueduct, he'd left Ledic with a broken nose and it had healed crookedly. On some faces that could've looked tough and handsome, but on Ledic, it looked sloppy and ugly.

Ledic headed toward the plant. He was limping.

Because I had twisted his leg in the ocean.

I headed home, my anger raging. Ledic had tried to kill me, and this time, it couldn't be chalked up to kids going too far. And I was sure that Walt Becket had been his partner, the one who'd shackled me. They were best friends who distilled their own liquor and got drunk every night. They had both married wives who stayed out of their way as they brawled over money, women, and any perceived slights. Ledic had been hired two years before me and while I'd been hired because the Town Council was thinking of what would be best for Corolaqua, he was hired because the Town Council was thinking of what would be best for Clearview. Making sure Ledic worked a hard job six days a week kept him out of wreaking even more havoc.

I walked into my house, thinking about my options. As if there were something I could do. I wasn't going to mete out vigilante justice, and going back to Hunter and Toric was a dead end. They'd been tolerant of Ledic for years. He'd beaten the crap out of a couple people and destroyed his fair share of property. But they'd never called in the Fibs and they weren't going to now. And the fact that it was Ledic who'd tried to kill me only reinforced that this was just a drunk bastard who'd lost control. *It was just like something that drunk bastard would do.* No way was this attempted murder.

Chapter Nineteen

SARAH CAME INTO the bedroom and told us that her dad had gone to bed. Then she snuck into the diner's storage building and stuffed Lily's backpack with food in case we ended up heading farther east than Black Rock. She asked for one thing in return. If we did come back this way, she wanted us to take her to the Territory. We said 'yes.'

WE WERE OUT of Sarah's trailer and under a triple tank truck before the cool night air had turned to dew. The driver was sleeping in the cab and the parking lot was silent. We'd picked a truck whose rigging was packed with supplies so, on the road, those supplies would keep us hidden from the eyes of other truckers.

An hour later, we heard the trucker step out of the cab and a few minutes after that, he came back and pulled out of the parking lot. Lily and I braced ourselves for the short trip to Black Rock.

TWO HOURS LATER, the truck slowed down and turned onto the Black Rock lakebed. There was no road here, just an endless mud surface. And as the truck picked up speed, it began to kick up massive amounts of dried mud. We had to shut our eyes to protect them. Every time I opened my eyes, I caught glimpses of dozens of other dust clouds. The trucks crossing the flats with us.

It wasn't long before every breath we took was packed with grainy particles of dirt. The lakebed was roughly four hundred square miles, so if our truck was headed all the way across it, we'd choke on these particles. I pulled my shirt up over my mouth to act as a filter and Lily did the same. But the particles were so fine and so relentless that they still made it through, and we both began to cough and wheeze.

Fifteen minutes later, all of it spent wheezing, our truck stopped. I figured we were somewhere near the middle of the lakebed, and I saw other trucks pulling in. But 'pulling in' was the wrong term. They weren't pulling into anything. The trucks were stopping in the middle of the most barren surface on Earth.

I looked over the wide expanse. The mud flats were covered with cracks, and the rising sun, low on the horizon, raked the cracks, turning the lakebed into a coppery mosaic of geometric shapes. Beautiful.

I shifted my focus back to the trucks. Some of the truckers had climbed out of their cabs, and the trucker closest to us was under his truck, prepping a discharge valve, as if he were getting ready to unload the water.

Unload it into what?

I heard our own trucker slam his door shut and realized that he, too, was headed for the discharge valves. The ones under *our* truck. If we didn't scramble out, he'd spot us. I saw him move past our tank, toward the back tanks. He was going to unload them first.

"We have to get out," I said, "before he gets to our tank."

"Where to?" Lily said, "There's no place to hide."

Talk about an understatement. We were on the flattest surface on Earth and surrounded by truckers. I looked around, trying to gauge whether we could run to another truck without being spotted, and that was when I saw the oddest thing yet. Under that nearby truck, a thick metal 'arm' was rising out of the dry lakebed. I looked over to another truck and saw the same thing, a metal arm rising from the lakebed. I glanced from truck to truck and saw the same bizarre scene playing out all over Black Rock and I realized that the trucks *had* pulled in to something. They'd pulled in to a water storage facility. Sarah's father had been right. Water was being stored here.

But why *here*? Why make this the transfer point?

I watched the truckers position the arms using controls attached to the arms themselves. They fastened the arms to the discharge valves on their tanks, tightened the couplings, opened the valves, and sent the water down through the arms. Under the flats, there must've been storage tanks as big and as numerous as those in Yachats.

Lily was riveted by the metallic arms. "Looks like trucks do come in from the east," she said. "Someone's got to haul all this inland."

"There's only one way to find out. We have to stay for the night." I turned my attention back to the nearby trucker. While the water was draining from his truck, he'd moved away to talk to another driver. "Those arms come out of hollows under the flats," I said. "The opening might be big enough for us to hide in."

"Sounds like a plan," Lily said, like she had no second thoughts about the danger.

But I wondered if the marauder whom Sarah had met had come up with the same plan, then been crushed when the arms retracted into their hollows.

Luckily, I didn't have much time to dwell on this scenario because we had to get out of the rigging before our trucker got to our tank.

I scanned the flats. Truckers were everywhere. So even though we only had to sprint about twenty yards, it was still likely that one of them would spot us. But we didn't have any other options.

"You ready?" I said.

Lily didn't hesitate. She grabbed her backpack and started to scramble out of the rigging. I followed and we raced across the flats aiming for the nearby truck and the arm underneath.

"A goddamn marauder!" someone shouted.

We ducked under the truck and the hollow came into view. Even with the arm protruding from it, the opening was large enough to dive into. We both jumped and I immediately felt panic. I didn't hit the ground.

I was in a freefall.

Finally, I hit and tumbled over. I scrambled to my feet, ready to run, my heart pumping furiously, and I eyed my surroundings.

Chapter Twenty

WE WERE IN a giant cavern. The floor beneath us was made of some kind of metal (steel?) and the arms rose from that metal and jutted out through rectangular openings above. From down here, I could see that the arms were aligned in an array. I was sure that we were standing on top of one massive storage tank and each arm fed into it.

The light streaming down through the openings created a checkered pattern on the floor, but the cavern stretched way past this pattern, into darkness, and I couldn't see where it ended.

"You going after 'em?" a trucker shouted. The voice was above us and it sounded harsh.

"Let's go," I said to Lily, expecting a trucker to drop down into the cavern.

Lily and I took off, running past the array of arms, toward the darkness. As we ran, I noticed that where the arms were connected to the floor, there weren't any seams or rivets. It was as if the floor and the arms were one huge piece of metal. That seemed impossible.

A shot rang out and the bullet clanged off the metal surfaces. I glanced up and saw a trucker leaning down through one of the openings, clutching a gun. He shot at us again and Lily and I both ducked behind an arm, but I wanted to get away from the openings, so I grabbed Lily's hand, waited a second or two, then took off again. We tried to keep the metal arms between the trucker and us.

Another shot rang out, echoing through the chamber.

Lily and I raced forward, weaving past several more arms.

A shot exploded off the metal floor as we hit the end of the array and ran into the darkness. Here, the trucker couldn't see us anymore but we couldn't see anything either. We raced forward and I expected to run into a wall any second. The cavern couldn't be too much bigger.

But we didn't come to a wall. I glanced back over my shoulder and saw that the checkered pattern was now fifty yards away. The trucker had stopped firing so we stopped running. We waited in the dark and didn't say a word. We wanted to make sure the trucker had given up.

While we waited I thought about the metal arms. I'd noticed that even though they were bent in four places, I hadn't seen any hinges, flanges, nuts, bolts, or screws. Not one piece of hardware usually associated with a joint. I'd also noticed something odd about the openings above us. There weren't any panels ready to slide over them and close them up, and I was sure the openings were closed when the trucks had pulled in.

AFTER THIRTY MINUTES of silence, Lily and I began to talk again and we laid out our next move.

Truckers would be arriving all day and unloading water. When night fell, we'd see if trucks came in from the east to load up. If they did, we'd climb up one of the arms and hide in the rigging of one of those trucks and see where it took us. And if no trucks came tonight, we'd wait two or three more nights and see if they came then. We had enough food to last about that long, but then we'd have to leave.

We had plenty of time before nightfall so we started to explore the cavern. First, we wanted to find out how large it was. We walked forward, farther into the dark, expecting to hit a wall any second, but we didn't. Our only landmark was the checkerboard of light behind us and it became smaller and smaller as we marched on.

"This place is huge," Lily said.

It was hard to believe that we hadn't hit a wall yet, and I added the enormity of the place to the list of oddities I was cataloguing.

Five minutes later, we finally hit a wall, and I ran my hand along it. "It's made of metal," I said and knelt down to feel where the wall met the floor. The bottom of the wall curved smoothly into the floor. "There isn't a seam here. It's like the entire cavern is one piece of steel."

"That's not possible, right?" Lily said.

I didn't answer. I looked back to the array, which was now just a tiny dot of light in the distance. How could this place be this big and still be machined from one piece of metal?

"Let's look for that equipment," I said. We had already concluded that somewhere down here there had to be machinery that pumped all this water back up from the storage tank below.

We headed back toward the array, the only area where there was enough light to examine the chamber. "Who do you think runs this thing?" Lily said. "It doesn't just take care of itself."

"Maybe there's a town near the flats," I said, but even though I'd volunteered that, for some reason, I didn't believe it myself.

BACK AT THE array, we walked up and down the rows of arms and didn't come across any equipment. We saw nothing but the smooth, unblemished surface of the metal floor rising into the arms.

We were also on the lookout for any truckers taking potshots at us from above, but the only things we saw up there were the bellies of trucks. Periodically, those bellies moved as truckers moved their second and third tanks over the arms. Then we'd hear the soft hums of the arms being repositioned. Those hums were as clean and elegant as the smooth surfaces around us.

After we finished exploring the lit area of the cavern, we debated whether to explore the dark outer reaches. We'd have to do it by feel because we wouldn't be able to see anything. In the end, we decided to hold off. So we hid in the dark, just out of sight of the openings, and listened to the trucks. Our wave of trucks left and the next wave pulled in, and that's how it went all day long. One wave after another, washing on shore, then retreating. We had plenty of time to talk and late in the afternoon, Lily finally told me the truth about her travels.

Chapter Twenty-One

LILY GREW UP learning biology. Her grandfather taught it to her and Lily had wanted to learn as much as possible. But her mother insisted that the tutoring stop and eventually her mother won that battle. That's when Lily started to pursue biology on her own. And it was during that time that she became interested in the Virus.

She started to research it, trying to hide her work from her mom, knowing that her mom wouldn't approve. Well, she was right. Her mom found her research, then tried to stop her from doing any more, and so began a series of bitter arguments. During one of those arguments, her mom let it slip that Lily's grandfather had studied the Virus and had abandoned his research because it was far too dangerous. By now Lily's grandfather had passed away, so Lily couldn't ask him about it, but she badly wanted to find his research. She tried to dig it up, practically taking apart the house, and she even searched other places in town where her grandfather had spent time. She couldn't find even one shred of his research, so she accused her mom of destroying it and that led to more bitter arguments.

If only Lily had connected the disappearance of that research to the disappearance of scientific knowledge in the Territory, she might've forgiven her mom. But like me, and everyone else in the Territory, she didn't connect the missing pieces of her own puzzle to the

missing pieces of the larger puzzle. Neither of us suspected that much more than ignorance was working to
destroy knowledge.

LILY ENDED UP wanting to develop a vaccine for the
Virus. A vaccine that would allow people to travel anywhere, anytime. To do this, she needed sophisticated
equipment and specific drugs and that was why she'd
begun taking trips to other towns. It wasn't to explore
the Territory.

   She traveled to dead towns that were once home to
hospitals or medical labs or biotech research firms.
There, she'd search for the equipment or drugs she
needed. Her mom was furious about the trips, but Lily
went anyway. And every once in a while, she'd find
the right piece of equipment or a drug or even some
relevant study that could help with her research. None
of this mattered to her mom. After Lily's first trip, her
mom stopped talking to her.

LILY MADE ANOTHER dozen trips over the years
and most of them were failures. Many of the hospitals
and medical labs had already been looted clean. The
biotech firms were usually better targets, and she
ended up finding enough equipment and drugs to continue her research. (On this trip, the one that had led
through Yachats, she'd been headed to a biotech lab in
Cutler.)

   When I asked if she was getting closer to finding a
vaccine, she said that she needed more information
about the Virus itself. At one point, she thought she'd
caught a lucky break when she came across an old epi-

demiological study. It'd been started right after the outbreak, but was never finished. And what it found was confusing.

Lily explained that there are two ways a virus spreads. Vertical transmission, mother to child, and horizontal transmission, person to person, like through air, saliva, or contaminated food. The Passim Virus was horizontal and that made sense. That's how pandemics usually spread. But what wasn't normal was the pattern of transmission. The Virus popped up in so many places at the same time that it didn't seem possible that transmissions between those places could've already occurred. Especially when you took into account another anomaly. The incubation period. If you became infected, you died within a few hours. From what Lily had been able to learn through the scant information she'd managed to dig up about other viruses, that was practically unheard of.

LILY ALSO TOLD me about her attempts to locate a good sample of the Virus. First, she had focused on samples stored in abandoned labs. It was a long shot that the samples would be still living, but a sample was a sample. She ventured out on four of these expeditions and each was a failure. The samples weren't where they were supposed to be. She said it was like following a fake treasure map.

So for the last few years, she had changed tactics. She'd decided to collect a sample from a recent victim, and that meant flirting with Mateo Ford, the guy who ran the Line in Klamath. Mateo was the key to finding out what towns were reporting new victims. When Mateo gave her information that she thought might lead to a victim, she'd head out.

But when she arrived in a town that had reported a death, the people there would always stonewall her. Sometimes they denied that there'd been a victim at all. She didn't know if the information Mateo had gleaned from the Line was just plain wrong, or if these people were lying because they didn't want outsiders to think the Virus had infected their town. Other times, she'd make it to a town and find that the victim had been cremated or already buried.

On one trip, where the body had already been buried, she asked the victim's family if she could exhume the body and take a tissue sample. They refused. And who could blame them? She was a stranger who'd snuck into town and for all they knew she was a marauder looking to spread the Virus. But the second time she rolled into a town and a family refused to let her exhume the body, she decided to do it anyway. It seemed wrong and macabre, but she was tired of failure. So she dug up the victim's grave, opened his makeshift coffin, and got a tissue sample. But when she got back to Klamath, she found that the sample had dissolved into the preserving solution.

So she tried again with another victim. And this time, she took a bunch of samples from the exhumed body, and some of those samples didn't dissolve. She tested them, focusing on a few biochemical processes based on what she'd learned about healthy tissue. She didn't have much to go on, but this was a start. She didn't expect a miracle, but she'd hoped to find at least a sign that the Virus had invaded healthy tissue.

She didn't. She worked on the samples for months and found nothing. She ended up more confused than ever.

UP ABOVE US, the daylight dimmed and the number of trucks dwindled down. On the cavern floor, the checkerboard of light softened. Night was falling and the temperature was dropping.

Just before sunset, the last of the trucks roared off and the arms began to retract into the cavern. They stopped just below the surface of the mud flats, then panels slid closed over the openings. These panels seemed to grow out of the ceiling itself and they left no seams when they locked into place, as if the ceiling had never had any openings at all.

The cavern was sealed tight, in silence and darkness, and we began our wait for the trucks from the east.

Chapter Twenty-Two

WE TALKED IN the dark and Lily told me the truth about something else. She said she didn't really think that the reason she was allowed to roam almost hassle-free throughout the Territory was her mom's influence as a Councilwoman. She was sure it was because someone with real power approved. Someone who knew she was trying to create a vaccine. Victor Crow.

I believed that. I knew the Fibs always enforced the law unless it somehow benefited them. And what could benefit them more than a vaccine that would make them immune to the Virus. Crow and the Fibs would have even more control over the Territory than they did now.

AFTER ANOTHER COUPLE of hours, we settled in for the night. We emptied Lily's backpack and used it as a pillow.

But I didn't feel tired. I was fueled by the adrenaline of anticipation. I stared into the dark and tried not to dwell on the creepy feeling I had, that I was stuck in a vast crypt, buried in blackness, sealed underground, far from home, forever trapped in the middle of a vast dead land. I felt like I had no past, present, or future. I tried to push these morbid thoughts away, but I couldn't.

AFTER ABOUT ANOTHER thirty minutes or so, I heard a hum. "Sounds like the place is opening up again," I said, and stood up, glad for the change of pace.

I looked to the ceiling, and the hum got louder but the openings in the ceiling stayed closed. I realized that the floor had started to vibrate.

"Let's move," Lily said.

She was thinking what I was thinking. A panel right under us was about to open up and we'd tumble down into the huge storage tank below.

The hum grew louder before we'd even gone ten yards. It sounded like a large piece of machinery was gearing up to do some heavy lifting. Then, past the array of arms, a section of the ceiling started to slide open and I could see that this wasn't going to be a small opening like the others had been. This was a large section of the ceiling. I watched it open until it was roughly thirty by fifty yards. Through it, the night sky was visible, inky black and sparkling with millions of stars.

"I don't see any trucks up there," Lily said.

The humming had stopped and we were once again engulfed in silence. We moved forward until we were under the opening. We stared up at the dizzying number of stars above us, captivated by the canopy of yellow diamonds.

Then I saw a shooting star, its tail brighter than any I'd ever seen before. And it didn't fade. It grew brighter, turning into an orange fire, then a burning royal blue flame.

And then it was right there above us.

A golden spacecraft.

Massive.

Lily and I instinctually ducked away from the opening.

I was stunned and my mind was grasping for explanations. The golden ship hovered over the opening. It was much larger than the opening itself so I couldn't tell how big it was.

Lily didn't say anything. I glanced at her face and saw the same feelings that were coursing through me.

Awe and terror.

The spaceship was silent. The engines that had propelled the golden craft down from the sky were as quiet as the Black Rock desert.

Seven cylinders descended from the ship's sleek belly. They grew directly from the ship, like metal limbs. Each cylinder was twenty feet in diameter and the color of fiery bronze.

Lily and I watched, transfixed.

The cylinders descended through the opening and into the cavern. I expected the floor to open up, but the cylinders touched down on the floor, and then I heard a tremendous rush. The sound of millions of gallons of water getting sucked up through the cylinders and into the ship. The floor *must've* opened up, but the whole process was seamless.

Lily and I looked at each other, speechless. We listened to the water. It was over in four minutes.

The cylinders retracted into the ship and, in a fraction of a second, the ship bolted up into the dark night sky. I watched the orange glow turn blue, then disappear into the canopy of stars.

The humming started up again, and the panel in the ceiling slid shut. We were in the dark again. But not about where the water was going.

Chapter Twenty-Three

WE DIDN'T EVEN try to come up with an alternative explanation about what we'd just witnessed. I told Lily that Crater must've known, too. He'd said, "That's not a star." He knew that some shooting stars were spaceships. *Space tankers.* He knew that aliens were stealing our water. *Earth's water.* And if Crater was a marauder, that meant that other marauders also knew.

We then considered the possibility that others in the Territory might know, too.

No one had ever spoken about it in Clearview. Not even a rumor. And if Benny had heard even just a scrap of such a rumor on the Line, he would've said something. Lily said she'd never heard anyone in Klamath say anything and she'd never encountered anyone on her travels who'd said anything.

But I did make one connection. From long ago. Something my father had said about water. "That's what you see when you look down from the stars," he'd said. Did he know that others *were* looking down from the stars?

WE HAD TO tell others. But we couldn't tell just anyone. We had to tell someone in authority. Someone who could do something about getting word out. I'd never be able to convince the Clearview Town Council. Because of my water theory, they already thought I was crazy and this revelation about what was happening to that extra water would definitely convince them that I'd gone off the deep end.

Lily had a better chance with the Klamath Town Council. Especially with her mother, the longest serving member of the Council. Lily had a strained relationship with her mom, but her mom knew that Lily was grounded in reality. She wouldn't make up something like this.

And *if* we couldn't convince anyone, we'd come back here and shoot video or take photos, though that'd be tough. We'd have to find a working camera and they were the rarest of Remnants. There weren't any in Clearview, and Lily knew of only one in Klamath, owned by the lone police officer. He kept it hidden and she wasn't sure it even worked. Of course, now we understood why cameras were rare. It wasn't just a coincidence. It was tied in with the water. *Everything* was tied in with the water. All the missing pieces of the puzzle.

WE LAID OUT our immediate plan. Tomorrow evening, as the number of trucks dwindled, we'd climb up an arm and hide under a departing truck, then ride it back to Yachats. From there, we'd make our way south to Klamath.

I didn't say it to Lily, but I'd go anywhere with her. Now that I knew that everything about the Territory was a lie, I'd start my life again. And if I could, I'd start it with her.

WE TRIED TO get some sleep, but ended up cycling through the dozens of questions running through our

heads. The first set was about the water mining operation itself. Why were the aliens keeping it a secret?
Wasn't their technology so superior to ours that they
could just take the water? Why set up the Territory as a
front? That night, we spun some complicated answers
to these questions and only later would we learn that
the answers were simple and logical and based on
straightforward economics.

We also had questions about the Fibs and the truckers and what they knew about the whole operation. A
secret like this would've had to seep out into the world,
even if it were disguised as a rumor. Somehow the
aliens had kept their operation secret from everyone.
But how?

We came up with a few answers and then went on
to other questions and other theories until the openings
above us slid open and the arms rose into the blinding
sunlight. Truckers maneuvered the arms, coupled them
to their tanks, and began unloading the water.

We waited all day. Wave after wave of trucks arrived, unloaded water, and left. Then the daylight
dimmed and the last wave of trucks began to leave.
Lily and I went from opening to opening until we
found the right truck. A truck with rigging and enough
supplies to camouflage us. We waited until the trucker
stepped away from the truck, then climbed up the arm,
and settled into the rigging under the third tank.

THE TRUCK DROVE across the dry lakebed, kicking
up plumes of dust, but this time we were prepared. We
had fashioned filters from the supplies in Lily's backpack. The truck made it to the road and headed west,
back toward the Territory. We had no idea whether it

would stop at the diner but, if it did, we'd already decided that we'd keep our promise and take Sarah back
with us.

But the truck rolled past the diner and into the
night. I felt bad about leaving Sarah behind, but I was
glad that she had her father there. I wondered if she'd
ever venture out on her own and leave him behind.
And then I wondered what she'd do when (if) word of
our discovery spread. Would she still want to leave?

On the trip east, Lily had been serene, her eyes
closed, and her fierceness in check. But on the trip
west, she was alert, eyes open, on the lookout for any
sign of trouble. That was because we'd come up with
an answer to one our questions from last night. How
did the aliens keep their secret? They murdered anyone
who found out.

IT WAS NIGHT when the trucker pulled into the storage facility in Yachats. He parked the truck near the
small building, then climbed out and headed inside. A
few seconds later, we scrambled out from the rigging,
ready to disappear into the woods behind us, but we
never had a chance.

Chapter Twenty-Four

THE FIBS CAME at us from both the front and back of the truck. There was no way of escape. Their weapons were drawn and they quickly surrounded us, then herded us over to a brown SUV. They shoved us into the back seat, then two of them climbed into the front. The four other Fibs loaded into a second SUV.

THE SUVS HEADED out of the storage facility and up into the hills, away from Yachats. Lily and I didn't say a word and neither did the Fibs. I looked over at Lily and she was staring out the window, not betraying her thoughts. I wondered if we were being held because of Black Rock or desertion or the destruction we'd left in our wake two days ago.

The SUVs pulled into a familiar parking lot. The lodge. The Fibs led us inside and funneled us through a neglected lobby, then down a gloomy hallway. We entered a den in the back. It was dominated by an over-sized stone fireplace and furnished with threadbare couches and lumpy easy chairs. One of the Fibs told us to sit down, then he and three of the others exited. Two Fibs were left guarding the door, their weapons at the ready.

I weighed whether to talk to Lily in front of the guards. I wanted us to be on the same page before we were interrogated. But I didn't have to make a decision because Victor Crow entered the room. He looked exactly like he had in Rick's basement, as if he hadn't aged a day. And his plain brown uniform still somehow looked more regal than any other Fib uniform. He strode over to us, tall and proud, and once again I noticed the only symbol of his power and rank. That silver belt buckle, a luminous mark of authority.

"Did I interrupt an important journey?" he said, standing over us, radiating that same menace from our first encounter.

We didn't answer him.

"You want me to talk first?" he said, a hint of a grin appearing on his face, "Okay. Seems fair."

Crow eyed me. "Two days ago, you completed repairs at a pumping station in the Swan Peninsula. Then, without a proper visa, you continued south. To Yachats, where you ran wild through the water storage facility, damaging a tank, and then disappeared into the wilderness. Why?"

I didn't have a lie ready to go and maybe that was why I went with the truth. Or maybe I went with the truth because somewhere in the back of my mind, I thought that by telling Victor Crow the truth, he might let down his guard for a fraction of a second and I'd be able to tell if he knew the secret of Black Rock.

"We were following the water," I said and met his eyes, searching them to see if my answer had triggered any concern. But his dark eyes were inscrutable. Telling him the truth had yielded nothing.

"And where did it lead you?" he said.

"We hit a dead end."

"You sure did," he said, then stood up and headed to the door, leaving me confused. Wasn't he going to interrogate us further? He passed the Fibs standing guard and said, "Take them out and shoot them."

"What?!" I said. "We're deserters, not marauders!"

But Crow was already out of the room.

The two Fibs stepped forward and motioned for us to get up. I was stunned at the turn of events. I knew that the Fibs were reckless and aggressive, but I never expected this. Crow *had* to know what was going on at Black Rock. That had to be the reason he wanted us dead.

USING THEIR WEAPONS, the two Fibs marched us outside onto the back patio. Six Fibs were already there, waiting for us, firing-squad style. One of them ordered us to stand at the edge of the patio and we did as we were told. Again, there was no way of escape, but this time it was do or die so I checked out everything around us, looking for a miracle.

Strung across the lawn, I saw the laundry lines, heavy with clothes, and that reminded me that families lived in the lodge. I had a flicker of hope that a mother or a grandmother or a sympathetic soul would see what was happening out here and run out to stop it. But I knew the reality. The odds were that these families, like most families in the Territory, were avoiding the Fibs.

The Fib in charge told us to turn and face the lodge. We did.

Then he shouted, "Weapons ready," and the other five lifted their weapons.

"Aim," he said.

The Fibs trained their guns at our heads, and I realized Lily and I had been dead from the second we saw that golden space tanker. I looked over at her. I wanted her to be the last person I'd see before dying. The fierce, lemon-haired beauty whom I'd fallen in love with. Our eyes met and a huge explosion suddenly rocked the lodge. Flames and debris erupted from the second floor windows.

The Fibs hit the ground like a trained unit, then flipped around, and pointed their weapons at the lodge.

I grabbed Lily's hand and pulled her off the patio and we ran across the lawn, ducking under the laundry lines. As we bolted into the forest, I heard the lead Fib barking out chaotic orders, but we kept running, stumbling forward in the dark and picking ourselves up when we fell. I wanted to get as much distance as possible between us and the Fibs and just as I was thinking that I'd have to spend the rest of my life doing that, we ran right into two figures. We scrambled away and I braced for gunshots.

Instead I heard a voice. "Let's go." A calm voice. Crater's voice.

Chapter Twenty-Five

WE FOLLOWED CRATER and the other man, whom we soon came to know as Tarkin Miloff, deeper into the woods. They knew where they were going, so Lily and I were no longer stumbling. We were moving fast and fifteen minutes later, we arrived at a dirt road and a car. Lily and I climbed into the back, Crater slid into the passenger seat, and Miloff keyed the ignition. We started down the dirt road and seemed to be heading even deeper into the woods.

"You know about Black Rock," Crater said.

"Why didn't you just tell me about it?" I said. I couldn't hide my anger. "You sent me right into the hands of the Fibs."

"If you didn't see Black Rock for yourself, you would've never believed it," he said, not reacting to my anger at all. "And as for the Fibs, they weren't part of the plan. They shouldn't have been in Yachats. Not yet, anyway."

"So that was an accident?"

"A bad one. Much worse than you know. And we'll get to that part. But right now, we want your help."

"Who's 'we'?"

As Miloff drove further into the hills, Crater filled me in. He and Miloff were marauders, *but* marauders weren't marauders. The Fibs had thrown that label on them. Marauders didn't plunder and loot. They were outsiders who knew the truth, and Crater told us more about that truth.

THE ALIENS UNLEASHED the Virus because there were just too many of us to control. They needed just enough of us to run the infrastructure for their mining colony, but not too many. Too many would mean the secret would get out and their perfect front would crumble and they'd have to use more of their own resources to mine our water.

The marauders had concluded that the aliens had perfected this system of mining water over millions of years and across thousands of planets. They knew how to exploit a planet's indigenous population without that population ever suspecting. On Earth, they used three simple techniques to keep their slave labor force from discovering the truth: Fear over the deadly Virus, absolute control of information through the Line, and the destruction of scientific knowledge.

And Crater told us that Crow and the Fibs weren't in on the secret. They, like everyone else in the Territory, were being manipulated. But for years the marauders couldn't figure how this worked. Why were the Fibs jailing and killing anyone who threatened the mining of water, if they, themselves, didn't know the secret?

The marauders got their answer when they came up with a way to tap into the Line. Once they were able to monitor the communications between the towns, and the messages going to and from the Fibs, they noticed something peculiar. Sometimes information appeared on the Line out of thin air, and that information was always false. Different kinds of lies built around one big lie: The Fibs had been led to believe that Black Rock was a reservoir that supplied water to the rest of the world. They believed this water traveled through aqueducts from Black Rock to ports on the coast of what was once Texas. From there, ships carried the water to surviving towns all over the world, and the Fibs and truckers were paid a premium to keep that water flowing and to keep the entire operation secret. They had no idea they were part of an alien mining colony.

This explained why rumors of other surviving towns made the rounds in the Territory. It stemmed from the lie that the Fibs were protecting. And that lie was the perfect front for the true nature of the mining operating. Let the slave labor force spend their time suspecting the existence of other towns rather than suspecting even a grain of the truth.

Crater emphasized the importance of the Line. He said that even though the marauders had been able to tap into it, they still hadn't been able to figure out how the aliens controlled it. And the Line was the key to keeping the whole façade going.

WE TURNED ONTO a tiny rural road and followed it for twenty miles or so. It turned into a dirt road which we followed until it ended in the middle of a forest even more untamed than the one we'd just driven through. From there, we began to hike through the woods and I broached a topic that I was sure Crater wasn't going to bring up himself.

I asked him about the salamander in the dirt. He denied drawing it, but I didn't believe him. And just as I was ready to press him about it, he launched into the story of Jonah Wolfe, the man who first discovered the secret of Black Rock.

Chapter Twenty-Six

JONAH WOLFE WAS from Port Huemene, a town on the southern tip of the Santa Barbara Channel. Port Huemene was a fuel town. Everything revolved around the extraction of oil and every family worked the rigs. It was hard and dangerous work. Before the Virus, the Channel had been home to twenty-seven platform rigs. After the Virus, it was home to four, and those four provided the fuel for the Territory.

After the crude oil was extracted, it was trucked south to Rapahanoc for refining and then trucked all over the Territory. At least that's what those who were privy to information about commerce believed. But the truth was that after the oil was refined, only some of it ended up in the scattered towns of the Territory. Most of it ended up in Yachats where tank trucks used it to fuel the transportation of water.

JONAH AND HIS brother worked the rigs, just as their father and grandfather had. By the time they were in their thirties, the brothers had worked all four rigs. Platforms Gina, Gail, Gilda, and Grace.

Platform Grace killed Jonah's brother. A thick steel cable snapped, swung violently across the deck and into his brother's stomach. It all happened in the blink of an eye and Jonah found himself holding his brother in his arms, trying to push his brother's guts back into his stomach. He tried to stem the flow of blood and pull the torn flesh back into place. But his brother died in his arms.

With a heavy heart, Jonah buried him.

And he didn't return to Platform Grace. Or to Gina, Gilda, or Gail. He wanted to run from Port Huemene. His brother had been his only friend. It'd been that way from the start. When Jonah first spoke, at the age of two, he spoke to his brother. His brother was four years older and he listened and answered. That had never stopped.

Those conversations had been enough for Jonah. He didn't need anyone else.

AFTER HIS BROTHER'S death, Jonah applied to the Port Huemene Town Council for a visa to leave town. He wanted to go to Obispo, a town with a handful of people. They farmed for themselves and didn't trade with other towns. Jonah figured he'd farm a small plot of land and on that land, he'd talk to his brother. Even if his brother never answered.

But the Town Council didn't want to lose Jonah. Oil rig workers were hard to come by. Not many people wanted to do those jobs. The Town Council denied his visa and told him to go back to work.

Jonah left Port Huemene, anyway. He journeyed north and somewhere along the way, he realized that there were a hell of a lot of trucks headed to Yachats. Trucks loaded with either gas, diesel, or water. So he traveled to Yachats and discovered the water storage facility. But he didn't know anything about the Territory's water supply and concluded that this must be the Territory's central water distribution hub, which made sense. What didn't make sense were the comings and goings of the double and triple tank trucks. They all left and returned within a couple of days. None of their trips lasted any longer. How could they be hauling water across the entire Territory? To him, it looked like they were hauling water to one location then coming back for more. So he stowed away in the back of one of the cabs and made it out to Black Rock and, there, he saw the golden space tanker loading up on water and bolting up into the infinite blackness of space.

Jonah didn't like to talk to others, but now he had to. He had to tell others that they were all part of a slave labor force. Slaves that mined water for an alien race. But even though he wanted to tell others, he didn't know whom to trust. He was sure those in charge already knew the secret and that they were protecting it. If he talked to them, they'd kill him. His solution was to find others like him, outsiders, people who wanted to leave their towns, but weren't allowed to.

Jonah would tell those people what he'd seen and if they didn't believe him, he'd bring them to Black Rock. He wanted their help. He wanted to free the Territory from the aliens. And most of all, he wanted to avenge his brother's death. He now understood that his brother hadn't died providing for his family and his town. His brother had died mining water for these aliens.

OVER THE NEXT few years, Jonah put together a group of outsiders. First, by taking them to see the golden space tanker themselves, and then, by setting up a base camp in the western part of what used to be New Mexico. By now, the Fibs were calling this band of deserters 'marauders' and considered them criminals and not just deserters. But this didn't stop Jonah from moving forward. He used his thirty years of pent-up words to inspire his followers to take on the mission of freeing the Territory and soon he and two dozen marauders began to implement a plan.

They needed cars and fuel, so they stole them. They used the fuel to create incendiary bombs. Jonah wasn't a scientist, but growing up in Port Huemene, he'd learned enough about gas and oil to build simple and deadly bombs. Bombs which the marauders would launch at the space tanker.

It took them two years to gather and build what they needed and, during that time, a few more men and women joined them. These newcomers were different than the people whom Jonah had recruited. The new arrivals came with technological and scientific knowledge and one of them even redesigned the incendiary bombs. They were drawn here because they'd managed to learn enough to suspect that something wasn't right about the Territory and they'd heard that Jonah Wolfe might know what that something was.

Jonah welcomed them. He knew that the marauders needed them. The enemy was far more technologically advanced than the marauders would ever be. He thought the new arrivals were so valuable that he didn't allow any of them to go on the mission to Black Rock. He feared that there'd be many casualties and he didn't want to risk losing any of them. He understood that, in the end, the marauders' most effective weapon would be knowledge. That was why the aliens had destroyed as much of it as they could without raising suspicion, and continued to wipe it out whenever it was rediscovered.

Jonah made a wise decision not to send those men into battle.

ON THE NIGHT of the attack, the sky was clear and the stars were crisp.

Jonah and the marauders drove their cars to the edge of the flats and waited. They knew exactly what time the tanker came down from the stars. So forty minutes before the ship bolted down, the cars set out across the mud flats. It would take thirty-five minutes to drive into position and five minutes to set up the bombs. They'd be exposed during that time, but there was no way around that. Jonah had timed it for minimum exposure.

Each car carried four marauders and each car towed another car. These other cars had their tops shorn off, their seats removed, and they carried massive bombs in the open cavities where the seats once were. Under each bomb was a launching device, and most of these launchers would target the belly of the ship, the part from where the fiery bronze cylinders emerged. Jonah thought this was the most vulnerable part of the ship. A few launchers had more power. They'd launch the bombs above the space tanker, and the marauders hoped that these bombs would rain down on top of the ship.

AT T-MINUS FORTY minutes, the marauders began their drive across the silent flats. Thirty-five minutes later, they stopped at the edge of the spot where the mud flats opened up for the space tanker. They unhitched the bomb-laden cars and drove the other cars back a hundred yards. Then they returned to the bombs and readied the launchers.

The mud flats opened up and the marauders looked to the sky and within minutes they saw the shooting star that didn't fade. They watched its bright yellow tail turn to orange fire and then burning blue and, like an all-powerful God, the golden craft was suddenly right there above them.

The marauders launched their bombs and sprinted back toward their cars. The bombs exploded on impact and the bottom of the ship was suddenly awash in flames. The orange fire clung to the space tanker, then spread in blazing waves across its underside. Seconds later, flames shot off of the top of the ship.

The ship was drenched in fire, flames falling to the ground.

Jonah and his men arrived at their cars and this was their moment of triumph.

CRATER TOLD US that he saw joy in his colleagues' eyes, but then suddenly everything turned. A blinding blue light engulfed everyone. The blue was sharp and clean and it covered the flats in every direction and, in less than two seconds, it vanished, like it'd never been there.

Jonah and the other marauders were gone. So were the cars.

Crater looked up to the ship. The flames were gone. The ship's sleek, golden body was perfect and the seven fiery bronze cylinders descended from its belly and into the opening.

The space tanker loaded up on water.

Chapter Twenty-Seven

WE HIKED IN silence. There wasn't much else to say after hearing the story of Jonah Wolfe. It was the story of the marauders' founding and it was a powerful story.

Lily broke the silence when she asked Crater why he thought he'd been spared that night. He had two theories, neither of which could be proved. It was possible that there was something about his physical make-up that had made him resistant to the blue weapon. Or there was a glitch with the weapon and that glitch had saved him. He'd never know why he was spared, but I could tell that there was something that weighed on him more than the question of why. You could hear in his voice that he felt terribly guilty for being the only survivor.

WE ARRIVED AT a cabin and Crater told us that this would be a temporary stop. Considering how deep we'd gone into the wilderness, I kind of figured that. He said we'd spend the night and in the morning I could decide if I wanted to help the marauders. I'd hoped he'd ask Lily to join, too, since that would make my decision easier, but so far he hadn't even hinted at that.

We stepped into the cabin, and the life I thought I'd never see again came rushing back. Benny was sitting at a table, his leg jittering and I'd never been happier to see it jitter.

"So you finally did a little exploring," he said, and headed over to me. We hugged, then all of us sat down and he filled me in on how he'd ended up here.

ON THE SAME night that Crater had approached me in the Swan Peninsula, Miloff had approached Benny in Clearview.

Benny had been exploring Colfax Junction, Clearview's abandoned train station. He'd pried open a rusted locker and discovered an old Internet Protocol manual inside. He couldn't believe his luck and as he headed back out, through the station, he started to flip through the manual, looking forward to reading it in its entirety that night. Every once in while, he'd learn something new about the Line from one of these old manuals.

He looked up from the manual and that's when he saw Miloff standing in front of the exit doors.

Benny started to run toward the back of the station and the abandoned tracks and Miloff shouted out, "Read this," then put a note down on a nearby bench and took off.

Benny, curious, stopped running and headed over to the bench. He scooped up the note and read it. By the time he finished reading it, he knew that whoever wrote that note understood more about the Line than anyone else in the Territory. The note explained how to decipher one of those mysterious data packets floating through the Line. Now he was much more excited about this than the Internet Protocol manual, and he didn't want to wait until the next day to decipher one of the data packets.

So he bicycled to the Town Hall, fired up the Line, and waited for a packet to come across it. The first few packets didn't fit the bill. It had to be the right kind. After two hours, he spotted one, went to work, and unlocked it. It revealed a code that promised to access a part of the Line that he didn't even know existed. He didn't believe that it *did* exist, but when he tried the code, it opened up a secret part of the Line and there he found another message waiting for him. It was an invitation to learn more about the Line. More than he could imagine. But he'd have to travel south and he'd have to leave tonight. Miloff would be waiting for him at the end of the Mory Aqueduct.

Benny didn't decide to go south right then, but he did decide to meet Miloff.

AT THE MORY Aqueduct, Miloff told Benny that there was a small group of people who knew more about the Line than anyone in the Territory and they wanted Benny to join them. But Benny was still undecided. Then Miloff told him that I wouldn't be coming back to Clearview, and it was because I was right about the water. That sealed the deal. At least, enough for him to go with Miloff and find out if I wasn't coming back.

BENNY SAID, "SO is it true?"

"I can't go back," I said, and told him why. I told him about Black Rock. But I didn't tell him there was another reason. Lily.

Benny asked me dozens of questions about the alien facility and I answered him as best I could. Then he asked Crater a question that I'd wanted to ask, but hadn't yet. Had the marauders ever told the Fibs what was going on at Black Rock? Crater said that they'd told Victor Crow, twice.

MANY YEARS AGO, Jonah Wolfe had sent a marauder to a young Victor Crow. This was before the marauders had discovered how to monitor the Line, so Jonah had no idea that Crow was being fed that big lie. Crow listened to the marauder's outlandish claim and, of course, he didn't believe him. But he did worry that this marauder could jeopardize the Fibs' high-paid work of supplying water to faraway towns. So he executed him.

Many years later, Jonah's successor, Will Xere, sent another marauder to Victor Crow, but this time with proof. Photos of the golden ship. But the photos were grainy and dark and because of the empty vastness of Black Rock, they also lacked perspective as to size and distance. The hope was that Crow would be intrigued enough to check it out himself, but he wasn't. He responded by executing this marauder, too.

It was after this that false accusations against the marauders flooded the Line. Accusations of sabotage and violent crimes. Threats to the stability of the Territory. So the Fibs started to hunt down the marauders and execute them. But the few who survived managed to learn something from this relentless persecution. They were on the right track. The aliens were manipulating Crow to attack because they feared the marauders could damage their mining operation. To Will Xere this meant that if he and his men could survive the Fib onslaught, they'd have a shot at freeing the Territory.

These false charges also led Xere to devise his first

great plan as leader of the marauders: Tap into the Line to get ahead of the charges. And that success led to the critical revelation that the aliens were also planting other kinds of false information on the Line. Information that secured their control of the Fibs and the Territory. From that time on, Xere and the marauders knew they'd have to pursue freeing the Territory on their own.

CRATER THEN TOLD us that Will Xere had been part of that second wave of marauders. A man with knowledge. Jonah Wolfe had known from the start that Xere was the smartest of that second wave and that he had the ability to inspire other men. Still, it wasn't Jonah who'd picked him as the next leader. He hadn't picked any successor. He didn't know he was going to die that night at Black Rock. It was the surviving marauders, the ones who didn't attack the space tanker, who chose him.

Crater told us that after many, many years of discussing and planning, Xere and the marauders finally came up with a plan to take another shot at freeing the Territory. And over the last ten years, they'd put everything in place. If we went with him to Iron Horse, the marauders' base camp, we'd learn about the plan and take part in it. But Crater didn't tell us much about Will Xere and I figured that was because the story of Jonah Wolfe was the tale the marauders bonded over. But I was wrong. There was another reason. A reason I'd learn from Xere himself.

Chapter Twenty-Eight

THE NEXT MORNING, I made my decision. It wasn't really that hard a decision to make. I was already a fugitive and I had nowhere to go. It wasn't a heroic decision, but a practical one. I'd go to Iron Horse.

Benny said he'd go, too, and Lily wanted to go, but she hadn't been asked. So she volunteered and Crater accepted, but I could see that he wasn't enthusiastic about taking her and I wanted to know why. About thirty minutes later, I had a chance to ask him.

We'd eaten a small meal and were hiking through the woods back to our car. Crater was up ahead of us, alone, so I caught up to him.

"You didn't want to take Lily," I said.

"You and Benny were cleared. She's an unknown."

"She must've been on your radar screen. She was on Crow's radar screen."

"I don't mean that we don't know about her. I mean we're not sure whose side she's on." I guess he could see that I took that personally because he backed up his claim. "The Fibs let her do what she wants, and they don't do that unless you're part of the team."

"Then why'd you say 'yes?'" I couldn't help sounding defensive.

"You wouldn't have come if I'd said 'no.' And my job was to get you to join us."

I couldn't argue with that. "But you don't really believe she's a threat, do you?"

"Who knows? It might account for what happened

in Yachats."

"What do you mean?"

Before he could answer, Lily and the others had caught up to us. I didn't want to have doubts about Lily, but now I did, so to combat that, I told myself that Crow wouldn't have ordered Lily executed if she was working with the Fibs. Of course, that wasn't as convincing a rebuttal as it would've been before I knew that the Fibs were so brutal that they executed marauders at will. Crow would have had no problem executing Lily if she no longer served his purpose.

AS WE APPROACHED the end of the trail, Crater told us that the trip to Iron Horse would be tough. The Fibs would be mounting an intense search for us. They'd want to kill the marauders who planted the explosives at the lodge. That was the most daring act of sabotage they'd seen in years, so aggressive that the aliens wouldn't need to manipulate them into hunting us down. From Crater's attitude about the blasts, I realized that they weren't meant to free Lily and me. They were supposed to be part of something else. Something that didn't go as planned.

We arrived at the car and Miloff, Lily and I climbed in. Crater and Benny hiked a little farther, to where another car was stashed. Then we all headed southeast, away from Yachats, in the same direction as the trucks headed to Black Rock. But we used different roads.

Three hours into the trip, we fell into a contemplative silence, and in that silence, I heard a low, steady thumping. Not the kind of sound I expected to hear in the wilderness. Miloff must've heard it too, because he glanced up at the sky just as two helicopter gunships swept over the hills and started shooting.

Bullets spit off the road and Crater sped up.

The helicopters swooped down and bullets clanged off the top of our car and shattered our back windshield.

Crater swerved wildly back and forth across the road, trying to avoid the gunfire. He couldn't plow into the forest for cover. The woods were too dense.

The helicopters shot past us, swung around, and came back firing. The hail of bullets was furious. Our front hood whipped open and flew into the windshield. Crater couldn't see and lost control of the car. It spun wildly, careened off the road, straight into the unyielding tree trunks, and came to a jarring stop.

The helicopters swung around for the final assault.

Crater was dazed, bleeding from the head, and Lily and I were shaken. But we had to get out before the helicopters finished us off. We tried the doors. They were smashed shut. So we kicked out the remains of the back windshield and I pulled Crater from the front seat. His pants were drenched in blood and from the look of it, one of his legs was broken. Lily and I dragged him out of the car and into the woods.

Benny and Miloff were already on the run, a hundred yards ahead of us. Lily and I ran, holding Crater between us, his dangling leg banging off the ground. Behind us, we heard the roar of the helicopters growing. They were landing on the road. Crater yelled at us to leave him behind, but we held onto him and kept running. I glanced back and saw Fibs entering the woods.

Crater ripped himself from our grip, crumbled to the ground, and yelled, "Get the hell out of here!" I hoisted him back up. Bullets thudded off the tree trunks.

Crater yanked himself away from me again and fell to the ground. I went for him and he commanded, "Go! You'll find what you're looking for in Iron Horse!"

I hesitated, not sure what he meant, and more shots rang out.

Lily shouted, "We have to go!"

We both took off and I caught glimpses of Miloff and Benny far ahead of us, disappearing behind trees, then reappearing. We raced forward, following them. Behind us, the gunfire slowed and I wondered if the Fibs had stopped for Crater. Then I realized that Miloff and Benny had disappeared. They were no longer popping out from behind trees.

We kept running forward and soon enough I heard the crunching of underbrush behind us. The Fibs were gaining on us when out of nowhere the ground beneath our feet dropped out and we tumbled down, hitting dirt. We quickly scrambled back to our feet. We'd fallen into a ravine, some kind of dry creek. I looked down the length of it and saw Miloff and Benny racing away. We ran toward them and they started to climb out of the ravine, back toward the Fibs. They were doubling back but, for that to work, Lily and I had to get out, too. So we hurried over to the ravine wall, grabbed some tree roots, hauled ourselves up, and scrambled out.

We lay flat on the ground, stock still, and waited for the Fibs. I heard them approach, drop down into the ravine, and then I looked up and saw Miloff and Benny in the woods ahead of us. They motioned for us to crawl toward them. We did. Then we all ran back toward the road.

But not all the way back. Once we closed in on the road, we ran parallel to it.

"What about getting Crater?" I asked.

"Not in the cards," Miloff said.

Chapter Twenty-Nine

WE MOVED AS fast as we could for over an hour, then settled into a hike.

Miloff was aiming for an abandoned resort. It'd been a marauder camp long ago and he'd heard that the former occupants had left a car behind. He couldn't be sure it was still there, but to get to Iron Horse, we had to hike in that direction anyway. If we were lucky, we'd make it to the resort by tomorrow night.

The helicopters circled over us twice and that slowed us down. We didn't want the Fibs to spot movement, so we stopped and hid under the thickest part of the forest.

While there, I asked Miloff about the attack helicopters and he filled us in. Crow had discovered four of them at a military base in what used to be California. No one knew how to fly them, so Crow taught himself and then taught some of his men. Miloff said that this feat more than any other had proved to Xere and the marauders that Crow was smarter than anyone in the Territory. He'd taught himself a complex skill based on knowledge that had disappeared.

THAT NIGHT WE camped without a fire so the helicopters wouldn't spot us. In the dark, engulfed by the sounds of animals on the prowl, Miloff told us his story.

The marauders had recruited him from Talahachee,

an electricity town. Talahachee ran the Orange Creek Dam and the dam generated power for towns in the central part of the Territory. Miloff was one of the workers who'd venture into the wilderness to fix transmission lines. Over the years, he'd developed a reputation for going beyond the call of duty. He'd fix lines that ran to abandoned homes outside of towns. He did it so people who didn't have homes could have them, and those people were thankful.

Then he started heading deeper into the wilderness, following power lines that hadn't been used for years. He could've repaired them, but no one wanted to risk going that far inland for a home. So instead of repairing them, Miloff decided to map them, for the future, in case people started to venture out again.

He went deeper and deeper into the wilderness, mapping out more and more of it. There weren't any detailed maps of the Territory and, back then, Miloff had no idea why. Of course, now he did. Maps were another way to decipher what was going on, so the aliens, through the Fibs, had long ago destroyed as many as they could. (When Miloff brought up maps, I remembered that map of the western states that I'd found as a teen and how I'd thought of it as a rare treasure. I'd been right on that front.)

Maria, Miloff's wife, drew the finished maps. She was an artist, not by trade, but by talent. Like everyone in Talahachee, she worked for the Orange Creek Dam. So she practiced her art by drawing these maps and they were striking. Miloff and Maria spent hours together. He'd describe what he'd seen, bringing his adventures to life, and she'd draw the maps from his stories and sketches. Their love for each other was intertwined with the maps of the Territory. Those were the children they couldn't have.

The marauders found out about Miloff from the Line. They saw the Talahachee Town Council send a communiqué to the Fibs, asking them to arrest Miloff for treason. They were accusing him of connecting a power line to a marauder camp, but the marauders saw that this communiqué had appeared out of thin air. The Town Council hadn't sent it. It was a false charge and that meant that the aliens wanted to get rid of Miloff. He was a threat to their secret. *But why?*

So the marauders wanted to get to Miloff first, to protect him, and to find out why he was a threat. They set out for Talahachee and arrived before the Fibs. They warned Miloff and offered him sanctuary, but they couldn't convince him that he was in any danger. Miloff believed, like everyone in the Territory did, that if you did your job and didn't rock the boat, the Fibs left you alone.

That night, the Fibs stormed his house and started shooting. They killed Maria and captured him. But he broke free and because he knew the lay of the land better than the Fibs, he escaped.

He camped in the wilderness for a few nights, contemplating suicide. He knew he could join Maria through death. Then he realized he'd already joined her. She was alive, out here, in the land that they'd mapped together. He felt her. Here, in the wilderness, he could still live with her. So Miloff joined the only other people living in the wilderness. The marauders.

Chapter Thirty

THE NEXT DAY we hiked at a fast and steady pace. There were no helicopters.

Under the purple glow of the evening sky, we arrived at The Cliffdale Resort. The wilderness had taken it over. Vegetation covered its cracked walls and grew on its roof. The decorative wooden beams that crisscrossed it were rotting and plants grew out from the rot.

We immediately started searching for the car and found it in the stable at the back of the property. The key was in the ignition, but the car wouldn't start. We checked the gas tank and it was almost full. But the gas had probably been diluted by condensation, so we needed a fresh supply of gas (assuming everything else about the car still worked).

Miloff thought there might be some gas stored on the property and we all began to search. We rummaged through the stable's underground storage area, the resort's maintenance buildings, the gardening sheds, and a half dozen other custodial areas, and came up empty. Miloff resigned himself to hiking to Red, a small marauder camp, where they'd have a car we could use to drive to Iron Horse. The hike to Red would take three days.

I told Miloff that there was still the possibility of getting the car on the road. I could try and separate the water from the gas in the car's tank. When it came to water, I was good at solving problems. I'd need some isoproponal, but considering we were at a resort, I knew the odds of finding some were pretty good.

MY FIRST STOP was the old housekeeping storeroom. Isopropanol had been a key ingredient in dozens of products before the Virus, including cleaning products. Sure enough, I came across a case of Windex, a mass-produced window cleaner from those days, and I saw isoproponal listed as one of the ingredients.

I sequestered myself in the resort's maintenance room and began to build a makeshift distillation tank. Meanwhile, in case my experiment didn't work out, Lily, Benny and Miloff gathered supplies for a hike to Red. I worked all afternoon and so did they. Then we all took a break for dinner. The marauders who'd used this as a base camp had left the pantry stocked with food, so our meal turned out to be a welcome luxury.

The food itself was a reflection of the marauders' determination to survive in the wilderness. Since their camps didn't have power, they preserved their food using the same methods that the small, self-sufficient towns in the Territory did. Salt, oil, sugar, alcohol, vinegar, drying, cold storage, and lactic fermentation.

After dinner, I finished building the tank and I distilled the isoproponal. Then I rigged up a spray dryer and turned the isoproponal into a powder.

I tracked down Miloff and we headed to the stable where I dropped the powder into the car's gas tank. Miloff keyed the ignition, but the car still wouldn't start. He tried a few more times and it sounded like the engine wanted to catch, but it wouldn't. We gave it a break for ten minutes, then I dropped in more powder. Miloff turned the ignition and the car started. For the first time since I'd met Miloff, he laughed.

We packed the car for the next day's journey.

WE EACH SLEPT in our own room that night. My room was musty, but comfortable. After the nights spent under rolling trucks and cold skies, my sleep was heavy.

I dreamt of trucks crossing the wilderness. Tank trucks. The roads they traveled were freshly paved, the asphalt sparkling under a brilliant sun.

But the trucks had no drivers.

Truck after truck rolled to the coasts. The brown coast of Africa, the green coast of Europe, the blue coast of Asia, and the gold coast of North America. The ocean levels were low and the beaches wide.

New desalination plants dotted the coasts, each plant molded from one huge piece of alien steel, like grand sculptures from a pristine future. The gleaming plants inhaled seawater and exhaled pure water. The driverless trucks filled their tanks with that pure water and headed inland. There wasn't a man or woman in sight.

I was watching the start of water's journey to the stars. A journey that didn't need the help of men. And when I awoke and my head cleared, I was left with one thought: There'd come a time when the aliens didn't need men to mine their water and when that time came, they'd kill the rest of us.

Chapter Thirty-One

WE DROVE SOUTH, over cracked and battered roads. Roads that Miloff knew would be free of Fibs and trucks. In some areas, vegetation covered the roads, but never thick enough to stop us. When we entered the redwood forests, the giant trees gave us complete cover. Even though I'd seen photos of redwoods, I wasn't prepared for their grandeur. All other trees were peasants compared to these kings. Under their protection, we drove the rest of the way to Red, a small marauder base camp consisting of three cabins.

Four marauders were currently stationed in Red. Their job was to make forays to the east, explore abandoned towns where the Virus was dead, and search for valuable Remnants. They brought those Remnants back to Red, and every few months transported them to Iron Horse.

That night, as I settled into a cabin, through the open window, I heard Miloff and the four marauders talking in hushed voices. There was an energy to their conversation, a kind of euphoric anticipation, and I knew they were talking about the plan to free the Territory.

At dawn, we filled the car's gas tank from Red's supply of gas and we headed southwest. Just before noon, we drove out from under the cover of the redwoods and into bright sunlight. By nightfall, we'd be in Iron Horse, a tiny town in what once was Plumas County, California. Plumas was a rural county where the Sierra Nevada Mountains met the Cascade Mountains and where millions of acres of forests met thousands of miles of rivers. It was a haven before the Virus.

We made good time and arrived in the early evening. The town was made up of just one small block of buildings, all two stories high. None of them housed shops like in Clearview or Yachats. Instead, they housed the marauders' operations, supplies, and, most importantly, their access to the Line. Iron Horse was hardwired to the Line and from here, the marauders monitored the entire system.

Miloff parked and led us into one of the buildings. Inside, a group of marauders was eating. Miloff pointed Lily, Benny and me to the back, where we grabbed plates, and served ourselves from bowls of food set out buffet style.

Miloff exchanged greetings with the marauders and they asked him about Crater. I saw their faces darken. They weren't prepared for the loss. Crater was a hero to them and I understood why. Even though I'd only known him for a few days, I'd felt his bravery and calmness.

As Lily, Benny, and I headed to an empty table, I thought the marauders were eyeing me. Maybe they were blaming me for Crater's death since he'd been sent to fetch me. But before that paranoia got the better of me, Miloff came over and said, "I want you to meet someone." I was about to find out that the marauders *had* been eyeing me, but it wasn't because they blamed me for Crater's death.

I headed out with Miloff and, in the car, I asked him what was up. He said I'd find out in a minute. We drove down Iron Horse's one street and back into the wilderness. We passed a few cabins on the outskirts of town and came to one which was set way back in the forest. It was an unadorned cabin at the end of long dirt driveway. Miloff drove up the driveway, pulled up to the cabin, and said, "Go on in."

"Who's in there?" I said.

"Will Xere."

"You're not going to introduce us?" I said, confused as to why he was delivering me to Xere.

"He knows who you are."

I STEPPED INTO the cabin. It was packed from floor to ceiling with shelves of books. The books dwarfed the worn couch, gouged coffee table, and two chairs which made up the humble living room. On the other side of the room, a large man stood up from a desk and turned to face me.

I was shocked. Emotions that I'd never felt before swept over me. I was staring at my dad.

Chapter Thirty-Two

HE HELD ME in his steady gaze and didn't say a thing. His eyes were filled with tears.

He looked older. Much older than the memories of him etched in my mind. He took a step forward and I rushed him and we hugged, tightly.

"Roy," he said.

I felt tears on my face. My tears. This was a miracle. A miracle I'd never let myself believe in. From the time I was nine, I had spent every day forcing myself to accept that my father was dead and gone forever.

"I'm sorry, Roy," he said.

I wiped the tears from my face and asked, "What happened?" And that question came from anger, not joy.

"I love you, Roy," he said. "And I hope that you can forgive me." He stepped over to the couch and sat down, then motioned for me to do the same.

I sat in one of the chairs and I couldn't say anything. Joy and anger were battling to control me.

"When the Virus hit, it killed most scientists, just like it killed most everyone," he said. "But unlike other survivors, the scientists who made it through didn't really have a chance. The aliens hunted them down and killed them. We still don't know how they did it, the Fibs weren't around yet, but they did it. Still, some managed to fall through the cracks."

"Like Lily's grandmother," I said, wondering if he thought Lily might be a traitor, like Crater had hinted at.

"Exactly," he said, without betraying his thoughts about Lily. "And like Zach Bell, a grad student studying physics at a school on the east coast. He was visiting his girlfriend in Bend, Oregon, when the Virus hit, so he escaped it and somehow escaped that wave of slaughter, too. Eventually, he settled down in Clearview and that's where I met him.

"I was a kid and by that time, he was a very old man. But he still remembered science. A hell of a lot of it. And he wanted to pass it on to someone. Someone who'd appreciate it and understand it. So he taught me what he knew. But Roy, he never put the pieces together. Probably because back then, it was all about putting the pieces of a society back together.

"Anyway, I was obsessed with what he'd taught me. And as the years passed, I kept learning more and then I figured out that something wasn't quite right about the Territory. So I quietly reached out to others, but not quietly enough. The Fibs were about to hunt me down when Jonah Wolfe offered me sanctuary. He offered to fake my death."

"Why didn't you ever contact me?" I blurted out. I wanted to hear more of his story but I needed to ask that question.

"I wanted to," he said. "And I kept promising myself that I would. But it was a risk. I knew you'd want to join me, Roy. You'd want to be a marauder. And that would've made you a target for execution. So I waited. And months turned into years."

"You sacrificed me," I said.

"I did, and that's why I don't expect you to forgive me."

"You could've come to me. Just once."

"I didn't."

I expected him to add to that. To justify what he'd done. But he was silent.

And so was I. I resisted the urge to cram all the missing years into this one conversation. I wanted to go back to the day I was staring out the window of our house, waiting for him to return home from Merryville. I wanted him to come home *that* afternoon. I wanted to start again from *then*. To live all those years with my dad.

He must've taken my silence to mean he could skip all those years. "I need your help," he said.

"You're going to attack the space tanker."

"No. We're going to take back control of the Territory."

WILL XERE, MY father, told me the plan. The marauders believed that if they had any chance of winning a battle with the aliens, they first had to tell everyone in the Territory that Earth was a mining colony. Once everyone understood that they were slaves on their own planet, then they'd band together to free themselves.

And the key was the Line. It wasn't just that the marauders could get the truth out on the Line, though that was part of it, it was that if the marauders could control the Line, the aliens could no longer use it to manipulate the Territory.

I learned that the heart of the Line was in Palo Alto, the Fibs' hometown. It was housed in a concrete building under the constant watch of the Fibs. And inside that building was a restricted area, an area that the Fibs, themselves, had never entered. All the Territory's communications ran through the routers, servers, and switchers located in that restricted area. Through that hardware, the aliens manipulated and controlled the entire Territory.

The marauders planned to enter that concrete building, and that restricted area, and destroy the heart of the Line. But when my father got to that part, I didn't get it. I asked him how the marauders were going to control the Line if they'd just destroyed it. His answer took me my surprise. It was the last thing I'd expected.

The marauders had built *another* Line, in Santa Barbara, a dead town close to Port Hueneme. There, the marauders had found a University which hadn't been stripped clean of its routers, servers, and switchers, and they'd used that equipment as the foundation for the new Line. The new Line used the old Line's infrastructure, all the cables already laid out throughout the Territory. But the marauders had looped it around Palo Alto. It had taken years to get it right and those mysterious data packets that Benny had seen were test runs for the new Line.

AFTER EXPLAINING IT all, my father stood up, walked across the room, and pulled a book down from one of the shelves. He handled it with reverence and I saw the title, *The Old Man and The Sea*.

"The old man was you," I said. "And the sea was the water."

"That's right," he said.

"You thought I'd understand that when I was nine?" Some of my anger was resurfacing.

"No, but I knew you'd get it later."

He was right. Somehow, it'd sunk in and helped point me to the water. "Like the four elements," I said. "You taught them to me just so I'd get that water was important."

"I couldn't tell you the truth. You were too young. But I had to lay the groundwork. I hoped that when you were old enough, you'd figure it out."

"I did."

He smiled. "I knew you would."

He put the book back. "I didn't want you to come to Iron Horse because you wanted to find your father," he said. "I wanted you to come because of the water. Because you wanted answers."

I could tell he was lying. And it was that lie that made me less angry. Will Xere, the marauder leader, may have wanted me to come to Iron Horse because of the water, but Will Xere, *my father*, wanted me to come so he could see his son before the assault. That was written on his face. My dad wanted to see me because he knew he might die in battle.

WE STEPPED INTO the cabin's small kitchen, and my dad opened a bottle of Curado and poured us each a glass. Then he began to cook dinner. Fried fish and potatoes.

The potatoes sizzled and that warm feeling from long ago began to fill me up. Love for my dad. But still, all those years of loneliness and sadness refused to move over. I remembered our last meal together. My dad had been quiet. He'd known he was leaving forever. "Why didn't you just tell me you had to go?" I said. "Why did you want me to believe you were dead?"

"If you knew I was out there somewhere, someday you'd come looking for me," he said. "I didn't want to risk that. It was setting you up to die." He pulled the potato slices from the oil and changed the subject. He asked about my life.

We ate and I filled him in. But when I took into account the last few days, filling him in about my life amounted to telling a simple story: I'd built on what he'd taught me and kept the promise he asked of me. To keep learning. Then I became an outsider because I'd learned too much. But I kept going and discovered that there was something about the water. And I was just curious enough about the water to head south to find answers. And I found my dad.

Chapter Thirty-Three

THE NEXT MORNING, Alek Sanders briefed Lily, Benny, and me on the assault. The marauders would launch the attack tomorrow night. The timetable had been pushed up because of Yachats. Originally, the marauders were going to detonate bombs in Yachats twelve hours before the assault, to draw the Fibs from Palo Alto to Yachats. But the Fibs had swarmed into town way before anything drew them there. Crater and Miloff had been as surprised as I'd been to find them in town. The only good part about the surprise was that those explosives were then used to free Lily and me.

The original plan called for the Fibs and their helicopters to be on their way *to* Yachats during the assault on the Line, but now they'd be returning *from* Yachats, if they weren't already back. But that was a chance the marauders had to take. Like Crater, my father believed that someone had tipped the Fibs off about Yachats. Now he figured the longer he waited, the greater the chance of the Fibs finding out about the real plan. But neither my father, nor any of the other marauders, accused Lily of being the snitch. Even if they thought it, they hadn't treated her any differently than they'd treated Benny and me. So far.

SANDERS TOLD US the assault on Palo Alto would incorporate four diversionary attacks on the town's most critical sites. The marauders planned to set off

explosives at Arastradero Road, where power lines
brought electricity into Palo Alto, at the El Camino
Reservoir, which supplied water to the city, at the Sta-
pleton Warehouse, where the Fibs stored their food,
and at Victor Crow's headquarters.

This was all in the service of getting as many of the
Fibs as possible away from the real target, the entrance
to the concrete building which housed the Line.

The logistics had been laid out weeks ago, but
Sanders added us in. Benny and I were going to be part
of the direct assault on the Line. With Benny, the marauders now had a communications expert who could
go in with them, which was why they'd recruited him.
They didn't want to risk sending in Sue Chen, the marauders' own expert. She had designed the new Line
and would run it, so was taking part in one of the diversionary attacks. If possible, the marauders wanted
Benny to find out how the aliens controlled the Line.
That information could prove to be valuable in the future. But he was told the priority was to destroy the
Line regardless of what information was gleaned during the assault.

Like Benny, I was chosen for the assault on the
Line. I wasn't a communications expert, but I knew
enough about technology and various kinds of equipment that I, too, might be able to figure out how the
aliens controlled the Line.

AFTER THE BRIEFING, over lunch, Alek Sanders told
us how he came to be a marauder, and I began to see a
pattern. When the aliens went too far with the wrong
people, or right people if you looked at it from our perspective, those people were driven to find the truth and

the truth led through the wilderness and to the marauders.

Before joining the marauders, Alek worked in the refineries. His job was to find spare parts for the refineries and when he couldn't find spare parts, his job was to construct makeshift parts. It took a smart man to design and construct those parts and Sanders fit the bill.

Sanders' daughter, Laura, worked on the shipping side of the refineries. She was smart like her dad and she helped monitor the oil coming in to Rapahanoc from Port Huemene, and the resulting gas and diesel going out to the Territory. After a few years on the job, she began to notice some anomalies, so she started to dig deeper into the shipping data, much more than her job required. Eventually, she came to the conclusion that somewhere up north, diesel was being stored. She told her father and a few other people in Rapahanoc, but no one cared.

Eventually, she went through the numbers with Sanders and he listened to her and agreed to talk to some truckers. A week later, Laura awoke at six, took a shower, dressed, and had her coffee. Her usual routine. Then she headed to her office, but she never got there.

At noon, Sanders learned that his daughter hadn't shown up for work. That was a first. So he went home to check on her, but she wasn't there. Then he walked her route to the office, but didn't spot her. So he walked it again, stopping along the way, checking buildings, yards, woods, and clearings, and he also knocked on people's doors. But no luck.

He kept looking and finally found her the next day. She'd been shot five times and her body dumped in the woods. He was crushed.

The local police investigated and the Fibs were

called in. The Fibs concluded that Laura had discovered where the marauders hid their fuel supply and before she could report it, the marauders had killed her.

Sanders didn't believe that for a second. He knew what Laura had told him. She'd never mentioned the marauders. So Sanders headed north to investigate and discovered that Laura had been right. Diesel was being stored in Yachats. And he saw that trucks were fueling up on it and heading east. Trucks loaded with water. He was sure that Laura, his smart daughter, had been murdered because whoever ran this operation wanted it kept secret. But who?

Sanders took a trucker hostage and got his answer. It was the Fibs. And now that he knew who'd killed his daughter, he sought out the enemy of the Fibs. The marauders. And when he found them, they told him who the real enemy was. Of course, he had to see it to believe it and when he saw the golden ship at Black Rock, he understood that his daughter had been murdered to keep the mining operation hidden.

Sanders had been one of the new guard, one of the men that Jonah wouldn't allow on the Black Rock raid. Jonah thought Sanders was too smart to lose. But Sanders was also the man who'd redesigned the incendiary bombs for the raid, so he was burdened with the guilt that the bombs had failed and all those marauders had been massacred. For him, this new assault was a second chance.

LILY, BENNY, AND I spent the afternoon learning how to fire machine guns and throw hand grenades. We weren't expected to use them, but Sanders wanted us to be prepared. Afterwards, Sanders told Lily she was going to be part of my father's team, the team that would attack Crow's headquarters.

I didn't like that we'd be separated and worried that there was a nefarious reason behind it. Maybe Lily, the traitor, was put on my father's team so he could keep the enemy close at hand, or worse. Maybe he and the marauders planned to kill her and they'd do it as part of the assault so I wouldn't know. I tried to convince myself that this was paranoia and focused instead on something else that was bothering me. Something I knew was real. My dad wasn't part of the team attacking the Line. Shouldn't he lead the charge? Wasn't he the leader of the marauders? Maybe the marauders had decided that they didn't want to lose another leader. Regardless, I lost some respect for him.

ALL THE MARAUDERS had dinner together that night and, afterwards, I spend more time alone with my father, in his cabin, surrounded by his collection of books. We focused on what might happen after the assault. He thought that if we destroyed the Line, the aliens would either abandon Earth or attack it. He had no doubt that they had some kind of economic formula which determined whether a mining operation was worth fighting for or not. And if they attacked, he was sure they still wouldn't reveal themselves. For some reason, that was paramount in all their tactics and my father hoped to find out why. Was there some Achilles' heel there? They'd use Fibs as they always did to hunt us down and kill us.

"And what if they abandon Earth?" I said. "Won't the Fibs still hunt us down? Crow's not going to believe that we blew up the Line to free the Earth from aliens."

"At first, he'll go after us," my dad said. "But then he'll see the difference in the Territory. He's smart. Without all that false information flooding the Line, every pattern in the Territory is going to change. And he'll definitely see that no one's paying him to ship that water anymore. He'll probably never accept *why* everything changed, but it won't take him long to realize that it *has* changed."

I agreed with that, but I saw a lot of unknowns. Too many. Still, I didn't challenge him. My bet was that he and the marauders had weighed dozens of plans, each with its own problems, and had decided that this one was best.

Chapter Thirty-Four

WE LEFT IRON Horse before dawn, traveling in a caravan of seven cars. The trip to Palo Alto would take six hours. We'd stop in Sunol, just outside of Palo Alto, and wait there until nightfall. We'd launch our attack at two a.m.

There wasn't much conversation in my car. The sun rose during our trip, throwing rosy light over the changing terrain. When we entered this part of the Territory, unlike up north, the wilderness ended and we began to travel through an endless landscape of sprawling, dead towns. Miles and miles of suburban towns that ran all the way to the dead city of San Francisco.

The marauders had scouted this route as safe from the Virus, but some roads were still littered with skeletal remains and dried-out, leathery corpses. The morning sun painted long stark shadows around the gruesome remains and I felt revulsion when I should've felt anger. This was more evidence that the aliens had committed mass murder to establish their mining colony.

WE ARRIVED AT Sunol, twenty miles from Palo Alto. Sunol had once been home to a National Park so we were once again protected by the wilderness. We'd be here for twelve hours and then we'd drive around the San Francisco Bay, past the salt marshes of the Bayland,

and up into Palo Alto.

We ate a meal, and then broke up into small groups.

Lily and I hiked away from the others. We hadn't been alone since Crater had rescued us, and I thought she'd want to talk about how her life had changed in the blink of an eye. But she talked about my father.

She said I'd received a great gift. A miracle. My father had returned from the dead. So why was I angry?

I told her that my father had abandoned me. How could I ever forgive him?

She kissed me and said that I'd have to find a way. Otherwise, I was squandering a miracle. She kissed me again and we watched the orange sun slide under the tree line. A ray of sunlight shone through the branches and caught Lily's hair, sparkling it lemon yellow.

NIGHT FELL, AND darkness engulfed Sunol. We all rested, but no one slept. At two a.m., we headed to Palo Alto. With our headlights off, we drove around the Bay, through more dead towns. The marauders had scouted this route for months and knew every inch. In the moonlight, I saw silhouettes of decay. Deteriorating buildings, abandoned cars, crumbling street lights and storefronts. These once densely populated towns were considered extremely dangerous, but the marauders knew that was a lie. These towns, like Palo Alto, were free of the Virus.

We arrived at the outskirts of Palo Alto and split up. One team headed to the power lines, one to the water reservoir, one to the food warehouse. The two remaining teams, including ours, headed toward the campus of what used to be Stanford University. There, my father's team would head to Crow's headquarters, located in an old administration building, and the rest of us would head to the Stanford Linear Particle Accelerator.

The Line was housed in the central building on the Accelerator grounds. In that concrete structure, electron beams used to blast atoms into tiny particles. My father found it ironic that a place which had once been home to advanced scientific research was now being used to keep the population of the Territory ignorant.

We wound through Palo Alto following the route mapped out by the scouts. We didn't see any Fibs. We drove into Stanford Hills, northwest of the campus, and parked our cars in a deserted neighborhood. Then we continued on foot.

My father, Lily and their team headed toward Crow's headquarters. Benny, Miloff, Sanders, Platt, Uli and I headed toward the Linear Accelerator grounds. We carried machine guns, grenades, and explosive charges.

We crossed Branner Drive, which separated Stanford Hills from the Accelerator grounds, then entered the grounds, a series of unkempt lawns and empty buildings. Only three of the twenty Accelerator buildings were in use. Miloff, who'd played this night over and over again in his head, led the way and we stuck close to the empty buildings, using them as cover. Up ahead, I saw moonlight glinting off the ground. That meant asphalt and that meant Pep Ring Road, which the Fibs used to drive through the Accelerator grounds.

Miloff motioned that the road was clear and we crossed it, then moved passed the Heavy Fabrication building, and headed toward the Metal Stores Shelter. We hadn't come across any Fibs, but that only made me more fearful. I thought that somewhere out there in the darkness, they were waiting for us.

We stopped at the Metal Stores Shelter. The entrance to the Line was less than a hundred feet away, across a parking lot and a grove of trees. To our right stood the Controls Building which housed Fibs. Once we began our assault, Fib reinforcements would come from Controls, but the building was dark for now.

WE HID IN the shadows of the Metal Stores Shelter and waited for the other teams to launch their attacks. If everything went according to plan, the Fibs would pour out of the Controls Building to respond to the strikes across town, and there wouldn't be any reinforcements left to protect the Line.

Across the parking lot, through the grove of trees, I saw the amber light from the entrance to the Line. Because of the trees, I couldn't see the entrance itself, but I knew that four Fibs were standing guard in that dim light, chatting, joking, and trying to stay awake. This entrance wasn't originally part of the building. It was constructed later, specifically for the Line. Double doors led to an outer room which led to the building's long inner chamber. The Communications Center was in that chamber, and the restricted area, the heart of the Line, was a little farther down.

During our briefing, Sanders had told us that the marauders had considered using the original entrance, but decided against it. It'd been barricaded long ago and was far from the heart of the Line. There were too many barriers and unknowns over such a long stretch of the Accelerator chamber.

WE ALL BEGAN to look to the east for the signal, a tiny flare. A yellow light, twinkling for a fraction of a second, indistinguishable from a star in the sky. It was the signal for the other teams to attack and for us to start a two-minute countdown. Within those two minutes, we hoped to see Fibs pouring out of the Controls Building, on their way to defend Palo Alto's critical sites.

Time, of course, slowed down as we waited, and just as I was thinking that something had gone wrong, the yellow flare flickered against the black sky. Miloff smiled at Sanders, then looked at his watch, and started the countdown. Miloff treasured that watch. It was a Remnant, a wind-up model, that his wife had restored.

We heard faint explosions. A good sign. The others had begun their assaults. I glanced at Benny and he was staring down at his machine gun. I knew exactly what he was thinking because I was thinking the same thing. We were both hoping we wouldn't have to use our guns.

My heart was thumping fast. I felt it in my throat and tried to will it to slow down. But the only thing that was slowing down was the time. Miloff looked at his watch again, then at the Controls Building. It was still dark. The Fibs hadn't been alerted. Miloff looked to Sanders and shook his head.

I heard more faint explosions and saw Benny's leg start to jitter. If the Fibs in the Controls Building didn't leave soon, we'd be outnumbered. My heart shifted into an even higher gear and I took a deep breath when suddenly, the lights in the Controls Building flicked on. I glanced at Miloff and saw relief sweep over his face.

Seconds later, Fibs poured out of the Controls

Building, ran to their SUVs, fired them up, and
screeched out of the parking lot.

They roared past us and onto Pep Ring Road.

We all pulled out our hand grenades, and waited
for the SUVs to round the far curve. As soon as their
tail lights disappeared, we left the safety of the shadows and sprinted toward the grove of trees.

We knew that the four guards at the entrance
would now be on high alert because they'd just heard
their colleagues race off. But that couldn't be helped.
Our plan was to attack immediately while they were
still confused about what the hell was going on.

Benny and I veered to the left and tossed our grenades over the grove. Before they landed, we launched
another set. On the far right, Platt and Uli did the same.
Miloff and Sanders hadn't veered off. They were
headed straight through the grove. The grenade blasts
rang out, one after another, in a quick symphony of explosions. Then I heard Miloff and Sanders laying down
machine gun fire and I started through the grove, with
Benny at my side.

I cleared the trees and saw chaos and destruction.
Two of the guards were down and two were stumbling, dazed and bleeding. Small chunks of the building's walls littered the ground and chalky dust floated
in the air.

Miloff and Sanders ran through the debris and into
the building. Benny and I followed, and Platt and Uli
were a few steps behind us.

Chapter Thirty-Five

WE RACED THROUGH the outer room, through a door, and into the inner chamber. We sprinted down the chamber, passing abandoned Accelerator equipment, huge and far more sophisticated than anything I'd ever seen. Up ahead, I saw a room built into the chamber. The Communications Center. And farther down, I saw a wall. A barrier. It ran all the way across the chamber and I knew that on the other side lay the heart of the Line.

Miloff and Sanders barreled into the Communications Center, ready to take on the two Fibs manning the Line. It was possible they'd deserted their posts, but we were pretty sure they'd never leave in the middle of a crisis unless Crow ordered them to. Benny and I continued toward the barrier and let Platt and Uli take the lead.

They arrived at the wall. There was a steel door smack in the middle, but it had no handles and no visible way of opening it. Uli looked it over, ready to make a quick decision. To me, the door looked as sleek and formidable as the alien facility at Black Rock. No way we'd be able to open it. Uli turned to Platt. "We go with the cables," he said, which meant he thought the same thing. No way to get through here in the next thirty seconds.

We all looked up, to the top of the barrier. We knew there'd be cables leading from the other side of the barrier to the Communications Center. Benny spotted them first. They ran along the chamber wall to our left, right above the Accelerator equipment.

Uli scrambled up onto the equipment and we followed. The cables ran from the Communications Center into a grate right in front of us. Uli took a second to assess the grate and I thought he'd pull out one of the tools he'd brought and pry it open, but in one powerful motion, he kicked it in.

We crawled inside and followed the cables through a ventilation channel imbedded in the concrete wall. The cables exited through a grate on the other side of the barrier. Uli kicked that grate out and we climbed out onto more oversized equipment, then scrambled down to the chamber floor.

I saw two distinct set-ups.

One, I expected to see. The servers, routers, and switchers that made up the heart of the Line, neatly ordered and effortlessly humming.

But next to it, I saw another set-up. Two large metal blocks, both bigger than any of the Line's hardware. They were rectangular, silent, and fiery bronze, the color of the cylinders that had descended from the golden ship. And while the routers and servers were adorned with LED readouts, screens, and switches, these monoliths were perfectly smooth. Not one seam or rivet anywhere along their gleaming surfaces.

Ten cables connected the silent monoliths to the Line's hardware and, as soon as I saw those cables, I knew that the monoliths were the aliens' Earth station. They were how the aliens controlled the Line. And us.

Benny focused on the fiery bronze blocks. No doubt, he wanted to study them. But our job was to find out *how* the aliens controlled the Line, and we had. They controlled it remotely, from somewhere across the universe. And now that we knew, Uli and Platt had to do their jobs. They placed explosive charges on the monoliths and on the routers, servers, and switchers, then set the timers.

We had four minutes to get out.

WE CRAWLED BACK through the ventilation channel, past the barrier, and climbed out on the other side. We raced through the chamber. Miloff and Sanders were waiting in front of the Communications Center, holding two Fibs at gunpoint. As we approached, they shoved the Fibs forward, and we all ran toward the outer room.

But when we got there, we ran into an unpleasant surprise. Twenty to thirty Fibs, weapons drawn, waiting for us. One of them shouted, "On the ground!" We didn't move and I'm sure they would've gunned us all down if it hadn't been for the two Fibs from the Communications Center. They were between them and us.

We had two choices. Get on the ground or engage in a firefight and get slaughtered. Sanders made the choice. He put his weapon down and started to lie down on the ground. I saw him mouth to Miloff, "Line's going down." He was right. In thirty seconds or so, the Line would be destroyed. We all followed Sanders' lead and, as we put our weapons aside and lay down on the floor, Crow marched in. But he didn't stop to bark out any orders. He continued past us and into the Accelerator chamber. Miloff whispered to me, "Crow's going down with the Line."

"Get up," shouted one of the Fibs. We did and the Fibs collected our weapons and herded us out of the building. They marshaled us through the grove and lined us up against the wall of the Controls Building. Lily and the marauders who'd gone to Crow's head-quarters were already lined up here. Except for my father. I didn't see him.

I looked over at Miloff and he was checking his watch. He looked puzzled and I knew why. The explo-sives should've gone off by now. Crow must've shut them down. But how was that possible? He couldn't have had enough time.

Chapter Thirty-Six

A DOZEN FIBS trained their guns on us. I glanced over at Lily and wanted to ask her what had happened to my father. Sanders, who was lined up next to me, must've read the worry on my face because he said, "The other entrance, Roy."

And he didn't have to explain anything more. I knew what he meant, and the respect that I'd lost for my dad was restored and grew tenfold. Will Xere was executing the back-up plan. A plan to get into the building through the original entrance. My dad was racing through the Accelerator chamber toward the heart of the Line.

Crow stepped out from the grove of trees and headed over to us. "Very brave," he said. His eyes reflected bemused anger, as if he admired our ambitious plan. He focused on Sanders and Sanders held his stare. Crow stepped up to him and it was all over in a flash. Crow raised his sidearm, shot Sanders in the head, and I felt blood spatter onto my cheek. Sanders crumbled to the ground.

Crow lowered his weapon, locked his other hand over his silver belt buckle, and scanned the rest of us. I was shaking, holding my breath, and I could feel Sanders' blood running down my cheek. I didn't move and didn't make eye contact with Crow.

I don't know what he'd planned next, to execute us all at once or kill us one at a time or send us to Devinbridge to rot in the penitentiary, but I'd never find out because right then a massive blast rocked us all. I looked toward the Accelerator Building and saw raging flames and thick smoke billowing over the grove of trees. My dad had reached the heart of the Line.

IN THE CHAOS that followed, we all ran. Some Fibs took off after us, but Crow ordered many of them to secure other areas of the grounds. I caught up to Lily, grabbed her hand, and we sprinted away from Pep Ring Road and into the dark. I tried to remember the layout of the grounds, but it was hard not to think about my dad. I was sure that the back-up plan hadn't called for timers and that he'd been killed in the explosion. That was why he hadn't sent another marauder in.

Lily and I ran parallel to the Accelerator Building, but kept to the shadows. Behind us, I could hear gunfire. I remembered that the Accelerator ran under the 280 freeway and thought we could use the freeway as temporary cover. Then, if luck was on our side, we could head south to the Jasper Ridge Biological Preserve. After the assault, all the teams were supposed to meet at its southern border.

We made it to the freeway and found Miloff, Uli and Platt already there. I looked back toward the grounds, hoping to see Benny running our way, but I didn't.

We started south. The original plan was to go back to Stanford Hills Park first and drive to Jasper Ridge, but now, we'd be hiking. After a mile or so, we had to leave the cover of the freeway and cross open land. I expected to see helicopters, but the skies were clear. We entered the north end of the Preserve and found cover again in the wilderness.

We moved through Jasper Ridge as fast as we could, until we arrived at its southern border. The other teams were there, minus five marauders including Sue Chen and Benny, the two we needed to run the new Line. On the positive side, the others had been able to drive here, so we had three cars.

Miloff debated with the other marauders whether to wait for Sue Chen and Benny, while I looked to the forest and thought about the sacrifice my dad had made. The plan hadn't gone perfectly but thanks to him, the first objective had been met, in spectacular fashion. No one would ever forget that blast.

Miloff and the other marauders decided not to wait. They didn't want to risk the Fibs tracking them down. So we climbed into the cars, and just as we were pulling out, Benny darted out of the forest.

Chapter Thirty-Seven

THE TRIP SOUTH had been mapped out by Miloff. He'd mapped it out knowing that the Fibs would be hunting us down after Palo Alto. The route avoided all towns (populated or dead), freeways, wide boulevards, and roads easily visible from the air. It was rural roads and the back roads of National and State Parks, all the way down to Santa Barbara.

I rode with Miloff, Benny, and Uli. The mood was somber. Miloff said a few words about my father, formal words about his sacrifice and his commitment to freeing the Territory. Then he looked me in the eye and said, "I'm sorry." Not formal words, but personal words from his heart. Acknowledging that I'd lost my dad.

Miloff then talked about Sanders, too, but there was a hardness to those words. A hardness that reflected his desire to avenge the cold-blooded execution of his good friend. He also spoke about completing the mission. He was determined to get the new Line up and running and, as he talked about that, I began to understand what he was feeling. Sanders and Crater were gone. My father was gone, too. The Jonah Wolfe *and* the Will Xere chapters of the marauders' story had ended tonight. If there was going to be a next chapter, it was up to us to start writing it.

OUR ADRENALINE STARTED to ebb and we settled into a quiet anxiousness. The night was silent. Dawn was a few hours away.

Miloff talked about the upcoming morning. The original plan called for Sue Chen to fire up the new Line at dawn. In towns up and down the Territory, the workers who ran the Line would come in to do their jobs and see what they'd always seen. The Line would look no different. But the first message they'd get would be completely different.

My father had planned to tell them to gather their Town Councilmen and once they'd done that, he was going to tell those Councilmen that the Territory was a mining colony set up to steal our water. Then he planned to call for a summit of all the Town Councils to explain what was going on. He knew that he couldn't just blurt out that aliens had enslaved us. The Councilmen would want proof. But by the time of the summit, the Councilmen would already have some proof. Trade would no longer be geared toward getting water to Black Rock and all those patterns would've changed. At the summit, my dad would offer to take representatives to Black Rock and show them the alien storage facility.

Now, if the aliens decided to attack, his entire strategy would be different. It'd be about organizing and defending. Ironically, that would be easier because the marauders wouldn't have to prove anything *and* the Fibs would help defend the Territory.

Miloff told Benny that it was now up to him to fire up the Line. If he couldn't pull it off, Town Councilmen would come in to work and be told that the Line had been down all morning. That had never happened before and there'd be panic in every Town Hall. We had to avoid that.

DAWN ROSE BLUE and purple, and the sun started to burn off the mist lingering on the road. We were closing in on Santa Barbara. The towering White Firs of the Los Padres National Forest were protecting us on the last leg of our trip, and I congratulated Miloff on mapping a safe route.

He said that we weren't home free.

Benny and Uli had fallen asleep, so I took the opportunity to ask Miloff a question I'd wanted to ask him the entire trip. "How many people knew about the back-up plan?"

"I didn't," he said, as if he were insulted that he hadn't been told. "I'm sure your father told Sanders and Crater. That was probably it. They were his closest advisers."

"Why didn't he tell everyone?"

"My guess is, he didn't want anyone to lose faith in the main plan."

I wanted to ask Miloff why my father hadn't told me, as if he'd know the answer. I couldn't help but think my dad had done it again. At nine, he didn't tell me he was leaving for good and, last night, he didn't tell me he might end up on a suicide mission. But I realized exhaustion was fueling my thoughts, and I focused on another question before anger took over.

How was it possible for Crow to disarm the explosives before they detonated? That was the real cause of my dad's death. If we'd succeeded, my father, Will Xere, would've never had to go in. Crow couldn't have had enough time to crawl through that ventilation shaft and that meant he must've known how to open that sleek metal door. And *that* meant he must've had access to that restricted area and knew about the bronze monoliths. He must've seen them before. Of course that *didn't* mean he would've jumped to the conclusion that they were linked to aliens. So what did he think they were?

OUR CARAVAN OF three cars entered Santa Barbara, a dead town, then headed west, toward the university campus. The new Line was located in Harold Frank Hall, a building that once housed the University's Computer Engineering Department.

Ten minutes later, after driving through empty streets, we entered the University campus. Gunfire erupted from every direction. We'd driven right into an ambush.

Chapter Thirty-Eight

AS SHOTS RAINED down on us, Miloff sped up, roared off the campus road, and onto a dirt lawn. Bullets pummeled the car and the windshield exploded, spraying us with glass. We ducked, but it was too late. Blood seeped from tiny cuts on our arms and faces.

Miloff drove the car across walkways and more dirt lawns. He knew the campus layout as well as he knew the Territory and he ended up under a covered walkway that ran between buildings. Bullets thudded off the walkway's roof.

"Grab the guns and follow me," he yelled.

Uli collected the guns and we all scrambled out and raced with Miloff toward one of the buildings. I heard a massive explosion and seconds later flaming debris cascaded down around us – metal and plastic – and I realized one of the cars had been obliterated. I hoped it wasn't Lily's.

We reached the end of the covered walkway, raced into the building, and down a decrepit hallway. Miloff led us down a staircase, but Uli yelled, "We'll be trapped down here!"

"There's a tunnel system connecting the buildings." Again, Miloff knew where he was going.

In the basement, we ran down a cinderblock hallway and into the building's mechanical room. We moved past a heat pump, toward the back wall and an iron door. Miloff lifted the wooden beam that served as a latch, opened the door, and we all followed him into the tunnel.

Inside, the dark wasn't like the dark of night. It felt oppressive. Miloff led, feeling his way forward using the pipes overhead.

A few minutes later, we exited the tunnel into the basement of another building. Then we made our way to the top floor. The building was ten stories high and we hoped to get a view of the campus and of the Fib positions. If we were lucky, we might also be able to see Frank Hall.

I DIDN'T LIKE the view from the roof. Two of our cars had been blown to pieces and thick black smoke billowed from their burning shells. Dead bodies lay nearby. I couldn't tell who'd been killed and didn't want to study the bodies to find out.

Miloff counted them. Three marauders were unaccounted for. But that didn't mean they'd survived the ambush. I held out hope for Lily.

Frank Hall was visible and we saw Fibs stationed out front. "The Fibs aren't going to destroy the new Line," I said to Miloff. "They want it up and running, like nothing happened in Palo Alto."

Benny added, "And you can bet they brought their Line guys and they're in there trying to fire it up right now."

Miloff asked us if we wanted to retreat, regroup, and let the Fibs have the Line. Maybe Crow would see right away that without alien control, everything on the Line had changed. Or we could storm in there right now, get it up and running ourselves, and tell the truth for as long as possible. We were outnumbered by the Fibs so we knew we'd only be able to control the Line for just a few minutes, if we were lucky.

But there was no debate. We all wanted to complete our mission. Go for the Line and get the truth out to the Territory. By now, every town knew that the Line was down and their Town Councilmen were panicking, wondering if the Passim Virus had swept through the Territory with a renewed vengeance.

WE HEADED BACK to the basement. The underground tunnels would deliver us right into Frank Hall, bypassing the Fibs out front. We'd end up about a hundred feet from the Line.

We snaked through the tunnel and emerged in Frank Hall's mechanical room. Miloff told us that if we had to fire shots to take over the Line, we had to make sure we didn't damage the hardware. Then he went to the door and listened, to find out if Fibs were in the hallway. He didn't hear any movement or voices and after a couple of minutes of silence, he cracked the door and peered out.

No Fibs. At least, none between us and the door to the Line, about seventy-five feet down the hallway. Miloff couldn't see in the other direction, but we'd have to live with that blind spot.

The plan was for Miloff and Uli to head to the Line with Benny and me in tow. They'd check inside the room for Fibs and, if clear, we'd all barricade ourselves in. But if Fibs were there, Miloff and Uli would storm the room and try to capture them without damaging the equipment. Then Benny would prep the Line for transmission. This wasn't the greatest plan, but it did have one good element. Surprise. The Fibs thought we were wounded, scared, and on the run, literally headed for the hills.

Miloff stepped out into the hallway, checked the blind spot and nodded to Uli. Clear. He started down the hallway and the rest of us followed. At the doorway to the Line, Miloff stopped and signaled to Uli – He made a fist and opened it, meaning the door was open. Then Miloff listened and it took no more than a second for him to point to his mouth. He'd heard voices and that meant Fibs were inside the room.

Miloff and Uli lifted their weapons, ready to storm the room. Miloff could've first peered in to see the Fibs' position, but if a Fib spotted him, the plan's only good element, surprise, would be lost.

They rushed the room and I expected to hear gunfire. Instead I heard Miloff shouting out orders to the Fibs, then he shouted for Benny and me to get in there.

We ran into the room. Miloff and Uli had their guns jammed into the heads of two Fibs who were flat on the floor, face down. Surprise had worked.

Benny immediately sat down in front of a bank of monitors and started tapping away on one of the keyboards. I slammed the door shut, but there was no way to lock it.

We all stared at Benny, waiting for him to give us a status report. I could see the Line was powered up. The Fibs had made it that far. The question was whether they'd sent out any transmissions.

"Nothing's gone out," Benny said.

Miloff looked pleased.

"But it's not ready to transmit," he said. "I gotta figure that out."

Benny typed furiously on the keyboard, and just as I was thinking we might have a little time before other Fibs checked in, I heard sounds from upstairs.

Benny looked up, nervous.

"Don't worry about them," Miloff said. "Just get the Line ready." Then he motioned over to me. "Take my position."

I stepped over to the Fib on the floor and trained my gun on him. Miloff looked at me and said, "When the Line's ready, tell the Territory what's going on. Straight up. It might be the only time they get to hear the truth."

He headed out, shutting the door behind him, hoping to battle the Fibs as far away from the Line as possible, to give us as much time as possible.

Benny typed into the keyboard. The sound of each tap was magnified by its significance. Then gunfire suddenly erupted from somewhere in the building and I heard crashing and heavy thuds.

"How much longer, Benny?" Uli said.

"Almost got it," Benny said.

Uli looked at me. "We can't let the Fibs get in here. We've got to go out there and keep them away, like Miloff did."

He was right. As soon as the Fibs stormed this room, it'd all be over. I motioned to the two Fibs on the floor. "What about them?" I said. We couldn't leave them in the room with Benny, and there wasn't enough time to tie them up.

Uli was silent. He didn't want to say it, but I knew what he expected. We'd have to execute them.

"We're ready!" Benny said, and pointed to a mic next to one of the keyboards. "Right here."

I stepped forward.

The door burst open.

Fibs poured in.

Uli shot at them and went down in a hail of gunfire.

But the Fibs didn't shoot at Benny or me. We were lucky. We were in front of the precious hardware and they knew they couldn't damage it. They rushed us, pushed us to the ground, then jammed their guns into the backs of our heads.

Crow marched in behind them and stepped up to the monitors. He looked the monitors over, then glanced at us and said, "You made some progress. Thanks for your help."

The Fibs who were originally at the monitors sat back in their seats.

"Can you run it or do you need some pointers from our prisoners?" Crow asked them.

"Give me a minute," one of them said, and started typing into the keyboard.

Crow moved over to us. "Pray that they need some pointers, so you get to live a little longer."

But I wasn't praying that they needed pointers. I was looking for a way to escape. Benny had the Line ready to go and, at any second, the Fibs would realize that, and Crow would bark out orders to kill us. From my prone position, I scanned the room but my vision was blocked by Crow standing over me. I looked up at him and saw that he was focused on the Line. Then I noticed his belt buckle once again and, right then, everything I'd seen over the last few days suddenly made sense. I saw how all the pieces of the puzzle fit together. I saw how the aliens could run their mining operation so smoothly in full view of the Territory. I saw how Crow had been able to access the heart of the Line in Palo Alto so swiftly.

"I'm ready to transmit, sir," one of the Fibs said.

"Kill them," Crow said.

I launched myself at Crow's legs, sending him

crashing down to the floor, then grabbed his side weapon, swung myself over him, and put the gun to his head.

"I know," I said, but I needed proof. I needed proof for the Fibs to stand down. Their weapons were all trained on me.

"You shoot me and you die, too," Crow said.

I wasn't going to shoot him. If I did, nothing would change. I'd be killed and so would Benny and then any marauders who'd survived the ambush. Then someone would take Crow's place, and everything would go on just the way it had since the Virus. And the years I'd spend without my father would've meant nothing. And the last two days I'd spend *with* him would've meant nothing.

"I know why you go along with it," I said to Crow, and I ripped the silver belt buckle off. It popped off with a sickening snap, like a human artery rupturing. Except that it wasn't an artery that had ruptured. It was a silver tube that ran from the back of the buckle into Crow's abdomen. A tube that transferred whatever was stored in the buckle into Crow's alien body so he could survive on Earth. The buckle was a machine as sleek and elegant as the alien storage facility, but unlike the facility, it was hiding in plain view.

Crow's body fell still and his eyes dulled. The skin on his face stiffened and started to pale, changing from a tannish pink, a human hue, to gray.

The Fibs lowered their weapons, stunned at what they were witnessing.

Crow spoke slowly, "I didn't want this job," he said. "Who wants to be light years away from home and alone? But I couldn't complain too much. I got a mining colony that was easy to manipulate. None of

you wants to know anything. You like being stupid."
His gray skin was turning white. "We'll set it up
again."

"But this time we'll know," I said. "It won't be so
easy."

"It'll always be easy," he said, "You can't change
what you are." His mouth stopped moving and his face
was now a lifeless mask, the color of white plaster.
Whatever was inside his human shell, died.

AN HOUR LATER, Benny sat at the controls for the
Line, his leg jittering, and I sat next to him. Lily was
standing behind me. We were the only marauders
who'd survived the Palo Alto assault.

Half a dozen Fibs were with us and one of them,
who'd seen Crow's transformation, had taken charge.
He'd told the others to stand down and I was grateful
for that. The Fibs weren't going to make a move until a
move needed to be made. Right now we were all on the
same page. Get the Line up and running, get the truth
out there, and prepare for the aliens' next move.

"Okay, go ahead," Benny said.

I leaned into the mic and I told everyone the secret
that my dad had wanted to tell me long ago. The secret
about the water.

24492432R00117

Made in the USA
Lexington, KY
25 July 2013